CITY OF DANCING GARGOYLES

TARA CAMPBELL

T0182431

sfwp.com

Library of Congress Cataloging-in-Publication Data

Names: Campbell, Tara, author.
Title: City of dancing gargoyles / Tara Campbell.
Description: Santa Fe, NM : SFWP, 2024. | Summary: "In the parched,
post-apocalyptic Western U.S. of the 22nd Century, wolves float,
bonfires sing, and devils gather to pray. Water and safety are elusive
in this chaotic world of alchemical transformations, where history books
bleed, dragons kiss, and gun-toting trees keep their own kind of peace.
Among this menagerie of strange beasts, two sentient stone gargoyles,
known only as "E" and "M," flee the rubble of their Southwestern church
in search of water. Along the way, they meet climate refugees Dolores
Baker and her mother Rose, who've escaped the ravaged West Coast in
search of a safer home. This quartet forms an uneasy alliance when they
hear of a new hope: a mysterious city of dancing gargoyles. Or is it
something more sinister? In this strange, terrible new world, their
arrival at this fabled city could spark the destruction of everything
they know. Tara Campbell summons fantastical magic in this kaleidoscopic
new speculative climate fiction"—Provided by publisher.
Identifiers: LCCN 2023053769 (print) | LCCN 2023053770 (ebook) |
ISBN 9781951631390 (trade paperback) | ISBN 9781951631406 (ebook)
Subjects: LCGFT: Dystopian fiction. | Climate fiction. | Novels.
Classification: LCC PS3603.A4833 C58 2024 (print) |
LCC PS3603.A4833 (ebook) | DDC 813/.6—dc23/eng/20231120
LC record available at https://lccn.loc.gov/2023053769
LC ebook record available at https://lccn.loc.gov/2023053770

Published by SFWP
369 Montezuma Ave. #350
Santa Fe, NM 87501
www.sfwp.com

To my husband Craig Hegemann,
whose love and encouragement built every city in this book.

I.

What is the point of a creature created for rain when there is no more rain?

"Do you remember?" M asks, shoving another clawful of sand away, and I say yes without even needing to ask what. I remember them well, the days when we didn't have to dig. When water came to us.

With the next sweep of his claw, M uncovers a fat, black beetle. I snatch it up and carefully bite off half before placing the rest into his mouth. We roll the tiny burst of vitality on our tongues until every last molecule of liquid seeps into our stone, then exhale the rest in twin puffs of iridescent dust.

Refreshed, I begin digging again.

"We used to just…" He gestures with his front paws, miming the torrents of rainwater we would simply allow to pass through us.

"I know," I say, now also imagining a storm, water first trickling, then gushing down through my body, then the skies opening up with so much rain, water wells up behind me and overflows, spilling down my sides and over my head. Soaking in.

Back then, we would stay damp for hours after the rain stopped. We actually welcomed the sun, craving its warmth after a downpour. Back before basking became baking.

M pokes a claw into a divot in the sand and pulls up another beetle. He gives it to me to bite in half. My eyesight is keener, my tongue nimbler, my teeth sharper—and he trusts me.

When we were still up on the church tower, I was around the corner from him, protected from the worst of the sun and sand-blasting wind, so I've retained more of my original features. M's hearing, however, is still keen. And he's the one who had the visions, a foretaste of the crumbling, the falling, the long, dry future before us. More than a century ago, he began foretelling these dusty days of want, and because I trust him too, we prepared, looking out from our perches to the north and the west, planning where we might go.

We were among the lucky ones, carved with complete sets of limbs. We were able to move around after the abandoned church finally fell. Granted, on the ground I'm not as graceful as I might have looked coiled around a rabbit high up on the parapet—for whatever reason, my sculptor added four stumpy legs to my long, sinuous shape. M's sculptor had more sense, endowing his powerful lion's body with wings large enough to lift him—and, conveniently, me as well. I'm light enough to carry, but M's also getting weaker. For the moment we're surviving, together. But up there on the wall, I couldn't have imagined how bad things would get. How deprivation would really look and feel. How thirst could hollow out an already hollow being.

The wind shifts a dusting of sand onto our heads from the lip of the hole. I look up and am startled at how deep we've dug. We'd been so intent on following the trail of beetles.

"We'd better go," I say. M nods in agreement. If the sand shifts and traps us, I doubt anyone would be strong enough to dig us out. If they even came to look for us.

M jumps and unfurls his wings, careful not to touch the sides of the hole. He pumps for lift while I wind myself up his leg in our practiced manner. This time I don't bother to coil around his whole body to distribute my weight because we're only flying far enough to ensure we won't get buried.

We touch down and begin the trek back to the church. This also is new—we used to fly back. He would glide easily, wings outstretched over scraggly creosote and spindly mesquite, far above dusty earth before it completely dried out, while I scouted out sources of moisture below. It was easy at first—we weren't selective, didn't care whether a trickle of water was muddy or clear, whether an animal was alive or dead. If carrion was too far gone, we could at least consume moisture from the flies or their offspring.

Now, a maggot would be a plump luxury; a stream would seem an ocean.

And so we walk, because even as brittle and light as I've become, I want M to conserve his strength.

As though reading my mind he asks: "Today?"

"Let's talk after we rest." We trudge back toward the remnants of the church. Those of us who remain have developed the custom of spreading out to forage in the morning, then returning to the shade of what little still stands in the hottest hours of the afternoon.

We settle in among the other gargoyles and doze, never quite sleeping. We were all fearful of resting at first, afraid we would succumb to exhaustion and desiccation and simply—cease. But we've discovered that rest is helpful, that we can close our eyes and pretend we're back in the time of rain. Opening our eyes to the early evening, with its break in heat, is a small gift every day.

This time, when I open my eyes, I look around at the others. "I don't see Vlad," I murmur.

"Or Beatrix," M says.

"Or Winsome," adds another gargoyle who has overheard us. "It's been days."

M and I look at each other.

We excuse ourselves for the evening forage.

"No story today?" Quasi asks, turning expectantly toward M.

"Maybe later." He barely looks at her before heading for the exit. M and I begin scanning for dimples in the sand almost as soon as we step out through the broken arch of the church door. It's much too close to find anything, but it's habit.

"Tonight?" he asks softly as we head away from the grunts of stirring gargoyles.

I open my mouth, but don't know what answer I'll give. We've never been more than a few miles from the church. Even when M had more strength he'd only fly so far that if anything happened to him, my stumpy legs could carry me back within a day. He's always been the more apocalyptic thinker of the two of us, but now, faced with the real possibility of leaving, I want to catalogue the dangers.

The problem is, I don't know them. Not exactly.

"Has anyone ever come back?" I ask, mainly to stall for time, because I already know the answer:

"Not that I've heard."

I stick my claw into a divot, finding nothing. "But maybe some of them have made it somewhere better now. Some have to have, right?"

M hesitates, probably also recalling the fractured, lifeless gargoyles we've spotted face down in the sand on our forays. "Maybe. Maybe the ones who left earlier would have had enough strength to make it somewhere else."

There's no way to know, no rules for this, since it was never supposed to happen—the church was never supposed to crumble from underneath us. We all sense that we're only supposed to go so far, but no one really knows what that distance is, or what happens if you exceed it. Only a few have tested the limits. Maybe they've made it to cooler, wetter climes—if there are any. Or maybe they're just piles of rubble now, strewn farther and farther from the church. But facts are facts: we've run out of food, and most importantly, I've run out of reasons we shouldn't go.

I sigh. With a nod, I answer him: "Tonight."

"Now?" M shoots back.

I hesitate. "Let's see how the forage goes." We both know I'm lying, though. We both know this is it.

The sun sets as M and I head roughly to the north—in our time up on the church, that's the side where moisture seemed to linger, where moss sometimes grew. At first it's no different from our usual routine; we normally wander all night on a forage. We dig and pluck, sifting through sand and sticks, sharing what we find. But as the black of night begins to fade, our silence feels different. M has never been one for idle chatter while we're foraging—he saves his stories for our free time back at the church, when everyone can enjoy them. Tonight, however, there is a brooding quality to his quietness. Instead of turning around in the dawning light to head back home, we keep walking without a word.

From: Manfred Himmelblau
To: Meena Gupta, Joseph Evans

Subject: Welcome!

First things first: Meena, meet Joseph. Joseph, meet Meena.

After emailing separately with each of you, I'm pleased to begin our work together at last. In this era of dwindling research budgets, *The Annals of Alchemical Changes* (previously *The Annals of Alchemical Testing*) has been increasingly reliant on talented, intelligent citizen scientists like yourselves to serve as Traveling Researchers. I am grateful for your interest, and I look forward to receiving your reports from the field.

Your list of locations to visit is attached. The precise order in which you visit them is up to you to decide based on conditions on the ground and the most effective use of your stipends. In terms of reporting, prior teams have preferred to collaborate on taking notes, but to trade off on writing and submitting reports. That arrangement has seemed to effectively distribute the workload.

Three things I must repeat from our previous discussions:

1) Our protocols dictate that this is an observation mission only. To ensure continuation of the modest funding we still receive, we continue to record active conditions on the ground, but have discontinued speculation as to who or what might have caused the changes in the environments you will encounter.

2) When you report for service in Portland, Oregon, you will be provided a hybrid solar/biofuel car for your joint use. The car will be outfitted with a kit containing basic health and safety items for travel

in the West (sunscreen, insect repellent, handgun, bear spray, etc.), but your best weapons are things you already possess: awareness and vigilance.

3) Most crucially: you must remain together throughout your journey. Your list of cities has been deemed safe for travel according to our most recent information. As with all alchemically affected areas, however, changes may still be occurring as we speak. Seismic activity and flooding (naturally occurring, as far as we know) have also introduced uncertainty into travel in the Western U.S. It is therefore of utmost importance that you travel as a team and be prepared for altered conditions and potential new threats. Wildfire season unfortunately lasts most of the year now, so please keep your air filtration masks handy—winds can shift quickly. If an area has become unreachable or appears to be dangerous, simply report the conditions and move on to another city. Your safety is the priority.

Please refer to the attached report for reference to previous work in this area. Certainly, I don't expect you to include citations in your reports—this was published in a popular science periodical. If you would like further information/access to cited sources, you will need to contact me, I'm afraid. Sadly, neither the original report nor its sources are available online anymore—again, delicacy of funding streams has caused many agencies to restrict distribution of their findings.

So, with that, Meena and Joseph, I will leave you to make travel arrangements to Portland. Our field officer there will have your gear ready. He will also provide a hot meal and comfortable beds before your journey.

Best of luck to you, and please contact me if you have any questions.

Sincerely,
Manfred

Dr. Manfred Himmelblau
Director, Citizens' Alchemical Realities Exchange (CARE)

Attachments: Itinerary_Gupta_Evans.PDF, In the City of Failing Knives.PDF

In the City of Failing Knives

"I cut you, I cut you, I cut you": Contemporary Wedding Customs in the City of Failing Knives
Popular Sociology, September 2112
Luisa Benevides, PhD & Jonathan Phillips, PhD

"I cut you, I cut you, I cut you."

These are the wedding vows in New Lucerne, Wyoming, the City of Failing Knives.

In this city, knives do not cut. They lose their edge as soon as they are used. You will sooner sharpen a knife down to a metal thread than get it to cut. Other things cut: scissors, razors, even the side of a fork or a spoon, but in this city, knives continually fail.

Not only do they fail to cut, but they go one step further: they knit things together. Take a knife to a cake, and the site of contact will bind into a dense, inedible seam of pastry. The rest of the cake will be salvageable, but you'll have to break the remaining pieces off a newly indestructible swath of sweetness right down the middle. Wedding cakes are cut with spatulas, which makes for easier serving anyway.

But before cake: the ceremony. The couple will stand before the officiant, staring into each other's eyes, receive prayers if that's their custom, recite poetry if that's their preference, be serenaded by a friend—whatever they choose. Then the couple will exchange rings and vows. Even in cases where couples have written their own, they always end in the traditional phrase: "I cut you, I cut you, I cut you."

At this point the couple will clasp hands and turn toward the officiant. A knife-bearer will approach the altar with the instrument (and here there is great variation: for formal affairs, the knife will be silver and filigreed, perched on a satin pillow; for rustic weddings, a hunting knife might lie in a basket of wildflowers; fantasy fans have been known to arrange for a sword-like knife to arrive stuck in a "stone" crafted artfully of papier mâché. Whatever the implement is, for safety's sake, it may only have one slicing edge, so as to be classified as a knife).[1]

The officiant will take up the proffered knife (usually from a toddler in a tuxedo, a cat in a bolo tie, or a dog dressed as a dragon, depending on the theme) and ask the couple if they wish to be knifed,[2] to which they must reply yes, freely and without reservation.[3] The officiant then raises the knife and utters the phrase again—a variation of "by the power vested in me by the [appropriate authority], I cut you, I cut you, I cut you"—then plunges the instrument downward toward the clasped hands of the couple, careful to not actually make contact. It is a delicate balance, because the more vehement the downward motion, the more potent the bond. The officiant must, however, stop before touching the clasped hands, to avoid the melding of flesh, or as in the infamous Atwood-Walters case, the severing of it. Because both power and precision are of such importance, many couples prefer to hire a professional officiant rather than entrust (and perhaps burden)

---

[1] For further background on the importance this requirement, reference the startling account of the Atwood-Walters wedding. The most comprehensive account to date: Johns, Edward. "Perilous Love: Wedding Customs in the Western Territories," *NewUS Cultural Studies* Vol 25(1):52-64 (2108). Fortunately, both parties responded well to surgery and recovered full use of their limbs.

[2] Many may wonder at the variation here—why the officiant says "knifed" whereas the wedding vows refer to "cut." This may be due to vestigial traces of linguistic convention that have carried into the current century. It is not difficult to comprehend how "I cut you" bears a greater similarity to "I love you" than it does to "I knife you," and may therefore be more reassuring to hear from a partner in the presence of sharp objects. Reference: Marks, Hailey. "Laughing All the Way to the Altar: Evolution of Ceremonial Vows West of the Mississippi," *Topics in NewUS Linguistics* Vol 12(1):13-20 (2097).

[3] Older variations on this practice will include a query to the attendees as to whether anyone has objections to this knifing, but in modern times this portion of the ceremony is rarely followed. Marks, 2097.

a well-intentioned but nearsighted pastor or a close but potentially intoxicated friend with the task.[4]

In rare but unfortunate cases where contact is made, and fusion occurs, hours of surgery and months of physical therapy may be required to achieve re-separation of limbs with full recovery of function. A tepid swing employed out of an abundance of caution, on the other hand, has been known to cast a pall over the rest of the day, and in some instances, has been cited as a reason for subsequent divorce, particularly when the union lasts fewer than five years.[5]

In one notable variation on the ceremony, no officiant is used at all. Each member of the couple instead takes up the knife and pantomimes stabbing the other in the heart three times, speaking the phrase "I cut you" with each false thrust.

Imagine what it would take to stand before the love of your life and open up your arms to absorb the plunge of a knife headed straight for your chest. What would it be like to grip that handle yourself and, in front of Deity and everyone, bring the blade down, aiming right at the heart of the person you love most in the world while proclaiming, "I cut you, I cut you, I cut you"?

Could you do it? Could you swing with all your might, knowing your future depended on putting your whole soul into the blow—and missing?

Could you stab with enough love to make it last?

---

[4] It was determined that the alarming error with Atwood-Walters was the result not only of improper equipment (knife-like sword instead of sword-like knife) but also of an officiant who had availed himself a bit too heartily of the prenuptial flask in the groom's dressing room. Johns, 2108.

[5] Center for NewUS Marriage, 20-year Survey 2090–2110, www.StayMarried.nuus/20yr

II.

We've been walking through nothing but sand dunes and tumbleweed for several days now, and in this brief time we've gone almost mute, our attention focused entirely on the search for sources of moisture and shade. When we spot another broken, desiccated gargoyle, we don't comment anymore.

Our days are shaped not by us, but by landmarks. If we find a stand of dead bushes, we stop to shelter in their scant shadows and pick at their bark for bugs. We travel in the morning, rest during the hottest part of the day, and set out again at dusk for another night of northward progress. M could likely travel faster on his own—he probably still has enough strength to fly without another gargoyle clinging to him—but he won't leave my side. I only hope he doesn't regret his decision.

Finally I can't take it any longer, all this change, this silence. I ask M for a story, like when we were back at the church.

"A story, eh?" M thinks for a moment, padding alongside me. "All right, here's a story some butterflies told me once. That's how I know it's true."

He goes quiet again, closing his eyes like he's listening to something inside him, even though he's hollow. Then he begins:

Our flight was already erratic. The humans smiled, commenting on our fluttering paths, admiring us as beautiful pollinators, but not as anyone they would want behind the wheel of a car. So a bunch of us got together and said, What the hell, let's lean into this thing and get wasted.

It's not a far leap from nectar to fermented fruit, just takes a little patience to wait for it. And not everyone was into it, but those who were curious gathered in the corner of the meadow by the old crabapple tree, and we had some drinks and some laughs. We laugh a lot, actually, even sober, but people can't hear us, so we didn't think they'd notice. And we don't know why they expected anything different, but butterfly-drunk is just chill. Of course once it was monetized, they wanted to know every last detail.

But we're getting ahead of ourselves.

We found out right quick that when we're drunk, flight's not just erratic, it's impossible. We can barely lift off a flower before pinwheeling right back into the grass. So we just decided to hang out, and it was all good until humans noticed us and began visiting. Then the farmer threw up a sign and started selling tickets, and people had to get even closer, trampling more of us than you could imagine while moving in for selfies. Being drunk, all we could do was lie there for days (newsflash, we don't have livers), hoping the social media princesses wouldn't wipe us all out, lying back for their boyfriends to snap away for all their #drunkbutterfly posts.

Some of us managed to get out in time, no thanks to all of the "butterfly shots" people bought for us from the farmer who owned the land. Few of us could resist the brightly colored "flavors," really just different food coloring dripped into the same old fermented crabapple mash by the enabler at the helm of Drunk Butterfly Farm. "Farm," he called it. The only thing that old fart produced for consumption was our dignity.

We were trapped—as too many of my brothers and sisters still are—dependent and helpless while visitors lifted our inert bodies, still alive but with reeling minds, and placed us on their knees or noses for their newsfeeds, just to throw us (or if we were lucky, place us) back into the grass while reaching for yet another, always seeking something shinier, more beautiful than what was currently in their hands.

Their entrance fees keep us in butterfly cocktails, docile and drunk. But we're not bitter—or, more precisely, we'd be bitterer if we hadn't first *observed humans, hadn't fluttered far above them and watched them go inside, far away from the sun, to type and talk and scribble things onto paper and sit and type some more, before plying their steady paths to different places, also hidden away from the sun, to sit and drink and tell stories of yet other places they wished they could be instead, then go home and sit and watch their storyboxes showing other, more beautiful humans flying more exciting paths to more bountiful fields than their own.*

Do not misunderstand us: we do not forgive humans. But at least we understand them. We know why they pay to come to Drunk Butterfly Farm, why they yearn for some magical, winged thing to remain still long enough for them to pick it up and toss it aside for the next, and then (and this is the part they only dimly grasp) to know that these beautiful discarded things can do nothing but watch them indulge in the luxury of walking away from it all.

We understand because it's a luxury that, with time and fortitude, we finally took for ourselves.

M ends his story and gives me that look that means he's just imparted a lesson. Perhaps he only means to underscore our wisdom in escaping, searching for a better world. But embedded in this story is another lesson, the same lesson all his stories hold: humans are bad. At their best, they are simple-minded, clumsy, and lazy. At their worst, they are evil, spiteful, and downright dangerous. Whatever type you encounter, according to M, beware: humans are not to be trusted.

I've stopped arguing with him. From our perch high on the church wall, some of them seemed nice. They would hug one another and smile, hold open a door, lean in to admire a baby in a mother's arms. But with his acute sense of hearing, he says, he's heard enough to know otherwise. And because they abandoned the town long before we fell, before we gained our full powers of movement and speech, we've never been able to meet one face to face.

We trudge on in silence, looking as always for the next bit of shade, until M lets out a soft grunt. He lifts his head to indicate the direction of some pale blurs on the horizon, then angles his steps toward whatever's shimmying in the waves of mid-morning heat over the sand. They could be trees, snapped short in a sandstorm, but there's something about the way their limbs are—

I gasp. "M, are those humans?"

"Impossible." He squints, though we both know my eyesight is better. "How many?"

"Two, I think."

They're wrapped in light-colored clothing, but even this far off, their bodies seem skewed out of proportion, their arms and legs overly long and ungainly. For a moment I wonder if the heat could be distorting them that much, but then I realize this is the first time I've seen them from the ground. They've always been safely far below my perch on the church wall. Now there's nothing between us but sand and heat.

"We could dig ourselves under," M says. "Play dead."

"Too late. They've already seen us."

I'm close enough to note that the humans have changed their trajectory and are now heading toward us. One is a little taller—not by much—and strides with purpose, loosing plumes of dust behind it. The other one walks slightly behind the first. "Maybe they can help us."

"Why would they?" M mutters.

"Humans created us," I say. "They have no reason to harm us."

M grunts. "Not all humans are the same."

He's right. Up on the church walls we heard all manner of human voices burbling below, some of them light and joyous, others bitter or fearful. But only M could pick out the details. He says he heard things so dark and corroded from some of them, he'd have run if we hadn't been attached to the building.

The taller one stops. Its features are unreadable in the shade of its wide-brimmed hat, but I can see enough to know both creatures are gaunt with light brown skin. The slightly shorter one has stopped as well. Its head is wrapped in cloth, and dark glasses protect its eyes. They could reach us in a matter of minutes if they started walking again.

"Well," I say, "the only way to avoid them would be to fly." But we both know M needs to conserve his energy.

I search his face for a sign. He flaps his wings and ascends while I wind around him in our practiced action. The dunes shrink below us as he arcs and heads north.

I can tell from his wingbeats that he's exhausted, incapable of taking us a great distance. He'll fly as high as he can, as quickly as he can, and use air currents to glide. I resist the temptation to twist and look back at the two figures we've left behind, or make any movement that will disrupt our flight.

Up here, with the wind in my face providing respite from the heat, I can almost pretend the world hasn't fallen apart—until I spot another gargoyle carcass next to a dried-up cactus below. All those failed attempts at survival. At least M's keeping us on a northward trajectory, and every fallen gargoyle we pass means we could be one step closer to a different fate.

Then I see it: a barn, broken and tilting, but intact enough to provide shade. I tap M to get his attention, and I don't even have to speak, because he banks right toward it. Our landing is a little rough—more of a fall. He'll need to rest for a while before we start out again.

We pick ourselves up and head toward the barn. Even in the few steps to the slanted doorway I notice that the sand is a little more like dirt in consistency, and scraggly weeds struggle up in tufts here and there. There must be some kind of moisture around.

We're about to step inside the barn when I spot a lump in the shadows at the very back wall. I stop, wrapping my neck and head in front of M to hold him back.

"What is it?" he asks.

"I don't know." It doesn't seem to have noticed us yet; hasn't moved. We creep forward. Still no movement.

I poke the lump with the tip of my tail and a cloud of flies erupts. If my mouth had enough moisture to water, it would.

I look at M, and he's already heading toward a discarded tarp. Together, we drag it over the dead animal. Even though the body is too spoiled to safely wick moisture from, there are enough flies trapped underneath to feed us for days. As my eyes adjust to the light, I see that a few of them are crawling out from inside. I'm still quick enough to get a few of them, and I'm relieved to note that the ones that elude my grasp always return to the carcass. I split the flies I manage to catch with M and we feast.

Once we've staved off the worst of our thirst, chomping and grinding, soaking in tiny amounts of moisture and exhaling the remnants in black puffs, M wonders aloud what kind of animal is under the tarp.

We lift the covering, knowing now that the flies have no interest in escaping.

"It's a dog," I say. Mangy and death-bloated, but still recognizable. I remember their tails wagging as they walked around with people in the before times.

M grunts. "Must have crept in here to die."

"Does that mean people are nearby?" I've only ever seen them with people.

Neither one of us has any idea. But the bounty here is too much to leave behind.

By day we feast on flies by the pawful, then scoop up their maggots when they hatch. This is the most food we've had since the rains fed us on the walls of the church. By night we explore the area, searching for any other sources of moisture that might sustain us when the corpse dries up. When I was almost completely desiccated, the clumps of brittle grass gave me hope. But now that my mind is clearer, I know that once the flies are gone, we'll need to leave as well.

I watch the skies, and every once in a while I spot birds off to the north. They don't look like the swallows that used to swoop around us. I can tell they're much bigger, given that I can see them from this far away. I tell M about them, tell him we were right to choose that direction, because if they're strong enough to fly, they must have enough to eat and drink.

M doesn't seem to want to talk about anywhere else, though. Whenever I mention leaving, he deflects with some observation about a tuft of weeds nearby, or a story from the before times, things I don't remember but he said happened when I was perched right around the corner from him. But, again, he heard more snippets of conversation on the ground below us than I ever could have. He could even hear the bats that would wing around the spires of the church hunting insects at dusk.

This is, he says one hot afternoon in the barn, how he heard about the City of Bingeing Bats. He tells me a whole long story about how they started out as regular bats, then started eating fruit, then discovered a taste for human blood and eventually sucked the whole town dry, and in the end, somehow, took over the entire city and live there now quite happily, human-free.

"But what do they eat now?" I ask. "Now that they don't have any more humans to feed on?"

M grins maliciously. "They go out and hunt. They can fly great distances, you know."

We both throw maggots into our mouths, and I think about how nice it would be to have a place to call home. "Do you think it's true? Do you think they could take over a whole city?"

"I don't know," M says, exhaling maggot dust. "I hope it is."

I wish I could explain M's dislike of humans. He was so beautifully crafted, his carver must have loved him. But then, he's heard things directly from their mouths. Bit by bit, he feeds me the grounds for his distrust, like the drizzle of water that used to spill from our mouths in a light rain: humans are greedy, they're weak, they're cruel and dishonest, they say different things inside the church than outside of it.

It's difficult to tell how much of this is true and how much is just M being M. Either way, with our current supply of food, I don't have a compelling reason to rush us out into the wider world.

FROM: Joseph Evans
TO: Manfred Himmelblau
CC: Meena Gupta

Subject: In the City of Glaring Chocolates

Transcribed audio of interview with Horace Lavaillou (HL), Proprietor, Conscious Chocolates, Hood River, Oregon

Location Notes: the river is now just a trickling stream, and rafting a thing of the past, but hiking and limited hunting opportunities still bring in enough tourism to support a small Main Street. Conscious Chocolates could more rightly be called Conspicuous Chocolates, the lone upscale boutique in an assemblage of outdoor outfitters and rustic eateries. A bell tinkles above us as we open the door into a gleaming white shop with glass cases full of trays of chocolates: dark, milk, white. All eyes swivel to the door…

HL: Thank you so much for visiting our small town, and for choosing our shop. I am at your service. Over here you'll find the crème-filled bonbons, over there the ones with nuts, and there the liqueurs. Everything is available in either milk or dark chocolate, with certain varieties in white.

JE: Thank you, and thank you for agreeing to be recorded. I suppose I'll start with the sign here—it says "glaring"?

HL: Indeed, that is the most popular question: why *glaring*? Why can't they simply *look* at you, or even more fundamentally, merely *see*? Well, if you were the one looking up at the world from your little paper doily, wouldn't you use any meager power you possessed to protect yourself?

Are you partial to citrus? This is a fresh batch of our orange peel and dark chocolate variety—isn't that a heavenly aroma?

JE: Um, yes, actually, it is. But back to the glaring. I mean—how?

HL: Ah, well, it was a matter of instantaneous evolution, you see. Spontaneous adaptation. When our great-great-grandfather Dr. Victor Lavaillou emigrated to the United States and began his experimentation, he was merely seeking to add another dimension to the gustatory experience. His dream: to create a truly interactive meal. He envisioned a banquet at which an amuse-bouche would truly amuse, gamboling onto the guest's plate, followed by salads that would flutter out from bunches in the center of the table to assemble themselves in individual diners' bowls. His experimentation with soup was messy, to say the least, relying as heavily on chutes and gravity as his dancing salads relied on well-placed fans.

His work eventually lost all favor when he progressed to the entrée. Wriggling noodles were bad enough, but it seemed no one could stomach a roast chicken parading about the table, peeling off strips of breast meat before dropping a wing here, a leg there, then dragging its carcass into a stock pot for consommé. It was too much. He was practically drummed out of town. His lab was locked up, then a mysterious fire destroyed his equipment and remaining records. Some say the fire was started by his own invention: a self-immolating crème brûlée.

But miraculously, one scrap of paper survived: the set of instructions upon which this whole town rebuilt itself. Nestled in this secluded mountain valley, his children and grandchildren quietly refined his technique, combining our world-renowned chocolate with his European flair, until voilà! Paris has its éclair, Vienna its Sachertorte—our tiny burg has its Glaring Chocolates: the world-famous Anstarrbonbons.

Would you like a sample? Raspberry crème perhaps?

JE: Perhaps in a little bit. But back to the original qu—

HL: Ah, right: why glaring, not merely looking or seeing? It's an existential question, really. If you knew you were created merely to be consumed, you probably wouldn't take very kindly to the organism that was so intent on snuffing out your life. You might even be angry that you were created with no means of defense—no limbs to fight or flee, no toxins to repel aggressors, not even the ability to elude predators via camouflage.

JE: So, are you saying they're—sentient?

HL: Sentient? That depends on how you define it. Plants and trees move, communicate, strategize, seek the advantage for their own kind relative to their environment, but would you describe them as sentient? Tadpoles develop legs to equip themselves for life on land, but would you say they do it on purpose? Such is the case with our Anstarrbonbons.

Are you sure you won't have a taste? Perhaps the sea salt and almond would be more to your liking?

While you consider it, please follow me toward the rear of the shop. Have a look here, please, through the glass into the kitchen. When our Anstarrbonbons first spring forth from the mold, their eyes are open and expressionless. See how they follow you, tracking, literally eye to eye, as though ready to bond, hatchlings to mother.

But now—there—you note the shift already, no? The brows that develop only to lower, the narrowing of the eyes, so slight, but enough to mark suspicion. They can read you, you see—and in this I include myself, because I am only human. They track our expressions, note our interest, and already this fresh new batch is aware that we find their kind delicious. It is not learned, as you see. There is no "mother chocolate" to teach them this defense. It is instinctual, an immediate wariness and perhaps, like an octopus shooting its ink, also a form of protection.

And over there is our finishing station, where each bonbon is lifted by hand onto a tray for the displays out front. We don't prepackage anything; we prefer to create each box according to our customers' exact wishes.

Speaking of which, might I interest you in a selection to take with you? Perhaps you will open the box at home, gaze down at the chocolates, and pick one up, tracking the way it tracks you no matter where you hold it. Perhaps you will brace yourself and place one of them in your mouth, recoiling at its twitch on your tongue. Or you might give the box away as a gift to become an uneaten novelty gathering dust on a shelf, Anstarrbonbons glaring vigilantly into darkness.

Or will you, as have so many before, simply leave the Anstarrbonbons behind while they stare through the glass of their display cases at the back of your head as you depart the shop forever? Indeed, this is why we were forced to begin charging admission to the shop, as distasteful as we find that practice to be. Most visitors never get farther than where you are now, staring at a tray of newborn chocolates, watching their gazes harden against you as they comprehend their lot, embittered (technically bittersweet) at the realization that they were created merely to be destroyed.

By now you've likely become philosophical, as we tend to do when we're planning to inflict damage, and you're probably wondering *Aren't we all? Aren't we all born just to die, created merely to be destroyed?* And you stand there, looking through a glass case into the dark, unblinking void of a doomed and glaring chocolate, wondering what it means that all you can think about is how delicious it would be to obliterate what stares back at you.

[END INTERVIEW: Expect chocolates for testing, sent via post]

FROM: Meena Gupta
TO: Manfred Himmelblau
CC: Joseph Evans

Subject: In the City of Falling Magicians

Transcript of audio interview with a resident of Salem, Oregon who would only identify himself as The Great Rodolfo (TGR)

Location Notes: We met this man in line at what locals call the Water Bank. The local university worked with the municipality to design quite an ingenious system: residents can earn credit toward their water bill by pedaling a bicycle hooked up to a generator that powers the city's watershed intake pump.

TGR: Long ago, it is told, cards fluttered upward out of magicians' hands. Rabbits floated skyward from their palms. Silk scarves slithered through their fingers into the air.

The trick was invented here, in this city, whence it spread throughout the society of magicians around the world. It was a simple illusion, one that made the observers think they were falling, if just for a moment; a trick of focus and movement meant to startle—how shall I describe it to you—like when you've stopped your car, but suddenly feel like you're rolling, and you grip the wheel and press the break before realizing it was the vehicle next to you that moved.

But what at first seemed a harmless sleight-of-hand kept surprising the magicians with unexpected variations, until they could no longer control it. They gradually lost the ability to hold on to anything, couldn't keep a newspaper or pen in grip, couldn't remember the last time they'd eaten soup, or rice, or anything that couldn't be firmly grasped between two hands. Even the pickles atop their sandwiches went zipping up into the sky; and one by one, the magicians' lovers slipped out of their embraces into space.

And this, as they say, was just the beginning.

Bit by bit, everything that was not these magicians began to disappear, ascending into the stratosphere: farms, pig by cow; woodpiles, log by spider; jungles, monkey by tiger; savannahs, elephant by baobab; until every ant, every pebble, every blade of grass, every speck of dirt and grain of sand, every drop of water rose from Earth's surface and hurtled into the heavens.

The magicians tried to hold down the strata of rock under their feet, but it was pointless: everything continued to fragment under their palms and float upward, crumbling skyward around them, silt flowing past them like snow in reverse, magma threading upward until there was nothing left but four hundred magicians from around the world pressed together in a knot of bodies, jostling to sort themselves out. For a moment they thought that was the end of the trick, far more than they'd bargained for, to be sure, but at the very least over and finished.

They couldn't believe this had all started with a simple illusion. Indeed, it began innocently enough, with gasps and hands clutching chests in those moments before smiles blossomed across relieved faces, until that fateful night when—and we'll never know how this could have come to pass—four hundred magicians around the world did the same exact trick at the same exact time, startling the planet into a chain reaction that began with annoyances of floating sandwiches and space-bound rabbits, but expanded catastrophically until the magicians were all that was left, a scrum of bodies in the middle of nothingness, relieved for a moment, wiping their brows, bashful but smiling, until they began to compress even more, squeezing into each other because now that everything else had flown up around them, there was nothing left to do but to collapse into themselves.

Only once these four hundred magicians had almost winked out did the planet comprehend the trick, blink, open-mouthed, begin to reassemble its magma core, chuckling sheepishly as it patted its layers of rock back on, sighing with satisfaction at the return of sand and soil and water and trees, smoothing its grass and animals back into place, and after a brief deliberation, taking its humans back too (though at times it regrets this, chalking it up to residual shock), and for one brief beautiful moment every person, animal, plant, rock, morsel of soil, and particle of air on Earth exhaled a sigh of relief and laughed.

Except three hundred and ninety-nine of the four hundred magicians. They cried, because they could no longer remember how to do the falling trick. It became a secret lost to time, and the last one who knew the secret was doomed to live for eternity, forbidden from sharing the illusion that might destroy the world once more, and for good.

They say this one last magician lives here now, in this very city. But who knows if this is true, if one person could carry for all time the burden of a tantalizing trick they may never perform, a secret they might perhaps speak of, but never reveal? Who could possibly be asked to contain such a thing?

I, for one, am certainly glad it is not me.

[END INTERVIEW]

[Quick question, Manfred: I know this is meant to be an observational mission, but can we get a little more context on what, exactly, the changes were supposed to accomplish? Not who, mind you—but is there something specific we're supposed to be looking for? A common thread?]

III.

As the days pass, our moods sink along with the dwindling population of flies and maggots. Have we miscalculated, eaten too many at once? I haven't seen the birds since we started out. What if there's no water where we're heading?

One morning I decide we can't just sit here like we did at the church. We were almost too weak to travel when we left. I won't make that mistake again.

I start my preparations to leave, hoping M will decide to come with me. I search the barn for something I can fashion into a sack for rations.

M eyes me, sensing my plan. "We shouldn't leave until the corpse is completely spent. Whatever we carry will just dry up."

"And we'll dry up too. We should set out while we've still got energy."

"We'll waste the rest of the—" M abruptly cuts himself off, holding up his paw to keep me from speaking either. He cocks his head, then points toward the door of the barn. I listen, but don't hear anything. M backs up slowly out of the light slanting into the barn and presses himself along a dark wall. I slink back and huddle next to him.

Then I hear a voice muffled by distance.

"It's a woman," M whispers. "And it sounds like more than one pair of feet."

"How many?" I ask.

M shakes his head and holds up a paw again. They're close enough to hear us now.

A different voice, slightly higher: "Ugh, something died in there."

"Put your scarf over your nose," says the first voice. "We've got to check for supplies."

I look at M, frantic. He loosens his wings and opens his claws. Mine never retract.

Two shadows step into the doorway, both dressed in baggy pants and loose, long-sleeved shirts. The taller one is wearing a floppy hat. The other has a shawl wrapped around her head. They stop just inside and lift their dark glasses, presumably allowing their eyes to adjust to the darkness like we did when we first came in from the sun.

M growls and I follow suit. I don't have the energy for a robust performance, much less an actual fight, but they aren't likely to know that.

The one in the shawl gasps while the slightly taller one reaches for something at her hip. "Where there's an animal," I hear her say, "there's food."

"What is that?" I whisper to M.

She's pointing something at us now, something long and black like the rods that used to gather lightning up on our church. She's going to break us to pieces with a bolt.

"Wait!" I yell. M tries to shush me, but I don't want to be exploded into chunks of stone. "We're not going to hurt you!"

The woman advances, still pointing the rod, the shorter person tucked up behind her.

"Idiot," grumbles M. "We could have chased them off without showing ourselves."

I sling my tail over his back to hold him, but he shakes me off and steps into a patch of light, opening his wings.

The woman stops and shields her eyes.

I don't really think before I step in front of M and rise up on my hind legs. He's right, we could have chased them off. I should be the one who suffers for my decision.

"Out," says the taller one, pushing the other one toward the door. "Out right now!"

"But it said—"

"It's a dragon. Out!" The woman turns and shoves her companion out of the barn in front of her.

Stunned, I stare at the empty doorway. Something glints in the sun at the threshold. I lower myself back to all fours and step toward the entrance. Outside, they're still running. The thing in front of me is metal, a container of some kind. I nudge it with my claw and sniff. There's liquid inside.

I look up. The people outside have stopped running. They've turned back around toward the barn.

"Is it water?" M asks. "Give it here."

"Wait," I say. The taller human is patting herself, frantic. The shorter one is holding the long black pole, looking between the barn and her companion. They're too far away to see details, but the cloth has fallen away from her face. She seems younger. I wonder if they're related somehow. Her daughter perhaps?

"What the devil are you waiting for?" M scoops the container away from me and tussles with the opening. I reach for it, but he drags it backward, out of my reach.

"Let's think about this. It's leverage."

M only grunts in reply as he grips the container between his paws and bites it.

"You'll break it," I say. "You'll spill all the water, and then where will we be?"

He snorts derisively but stops chewing.

I use the pause to get closer. "They had water. And they know where to get more."

"Why do you trust them?" he asks, looking around me out toward the humans.

I turn to look with him. They're still staring at our barn, the woman's hand covering her mouth.

With a sigh, I ask him, "Do we have a choice?"

IV.

Mama stands still for a long while, hand over her mouth. She doesn't like when I interrupt her while she's thinking, so I hold her spear and wait for her to tell us what comes next.

I'm thirsty, but I'm sure I'm just noticing it more now because she's worried about the canteen she dropped. I'm just glad it wasn't me who lost half our remaining water.

What I want to say is *It's not your fault*, or *We've still got mine,* but what I decide on is, "Was that really a dragon?"

She cuts me a brief sidelong look before turning her attention back to the barn. "Use your head, girl. Wings, claws, serpent-like body. Those teeth."

I lift my sunglasses and squint, trying to get a better look at the creature—creatures?—messing around with our water inside the barn. "I've never seen one up close, is all. And I didn't know they talk." Plus, I could swear there's more than one animal in there.

Mama's lips press tight. "Dragons are different in different places. You know how they were. Didn't care about the people who lived in the test sites."

She's talking about the government again, their secret weapons testing decades ago. Nothing has been the same since, she says; and I just have to imagine it because in my almost eighteen years, this is the only way I've ever known it. I suppose it must have been pretty terrifying to have all the lizards around you turn into dragons from one year to the next, or watch wolves float, or see statues sailing or whatever. She never talks about it.

"Let's just go, then," I say.

"We don't have enough."

She's right. Although our canteens distill moisture from the air, without both of them we won't have enough water to reach Carson City.

I lean the spear toward her, and she takes it from my hand. Then I unsheathe my dagger and take a deep breath in and out, clenching my teeth to keep steady.

"It's small," she says. "If it breathes fire, we'll go."

She holds the spear tip forward and I stay one step behind her as we approach the barn, both of us slightly crouched, knees bent, ready to spring in any direction. I hold my breath. The only sound is the crinkle of scraggly weeds beneath our feet. The inside of the barn is rank and shadowy, but I'm close enough to the entrance to make out two distinct figures inside. They stop whatever they were doing to watch us. I halt, and Mama does too.

One of the figures steps out of the barn into the light: a long, grey, serpent creature with four legs attached to a scaly body. It has a long snout with a forked tongue darting out from between rows of sharp-looking teeth. Even though it just moved, it looks like it's made of stone.

Mama steps directly in front of me, forcing me to lean to the side to see the creature. It's standing in front of the barn looking at us out of its bulbous round eyes. Its stance doesn't seem hostile. It's not crouched like we are, and its long, pointy ears are swiveling, like it's listening.

"We don't mean you any harm," it says, its voice rasping like gravel. It nudges our canteen with a leg, more to focus our attention on it than to move it closer to us. "This is yours."

This isn't a question, but an acknowledgment of our need.

"Where are you going?" it asks.

I step out from behind Mama for a better look—I suppose the creature's wide-open eyes could mean wildness, but somehow they don't read that way to me—and she sticks her arm in front of me as though that could protect me.

"Where are you traveling to?" it asks again, louder. It's "t"s clack like tiny rockslides.

I start to speak, but Mama pipes up: "We're heading south."

The second creature emerges from the barn, and we both shrink back from the lion-like creature striding on muscular legs, baring its teeth. It doesn't unfurl its wings, just raises and settles them slightly as though to remind us it has them. It's made of the same grey stone.

"We saw you before," it said. "Why are you lying?"

The four-legged serpent looks down briefly. There's something calm about it, unlike the winged lion bristling next to it.

"You're heading north," the snake-thing says, again not a question.

Mama takes a deep breath, and a long time exhaling. "Yes."

"There's water there?"

Another deep breath. "Yes."

The serpent's tail twitches. "We will travel with you," it says, looping its tail through the canteen's strap.

"We don't have enough water for four," Mama argues.

"Without this," the creature says, lifting the canteen, "you don't have enough water for two."

I can tell she's more pissed than scared. After all her planning to get us out of Oakland when it flooded, then out of LA after the big earthquake, then out of Joshua Tree while it burned, now we're stuck here: sunbaked, covered in grit, rationing protein bars, and staring down stone animals in a barn over our own water with only a spear and a dagger to defend ourselves. This was not the plan.

But then, what choice do we have?

Mama nods and, without a word, turns to head in the direction we've been traveling these past weeks. I lengthen a couple of steps to reach her side. Behind us: the crunch of footsteps, the sweep of a serpent's tail over gritty soil. I glance back, see the canteen swinging from the snake-beast's neck, the flutter of the lion's wings settling against its flanks.

Our steps settle into a sloughing rhythm as we head north to Carson City.

FROM: Joseph Evans
TO: Manfred Himmelblau
CC: Meena Gupta

Subject: In the City of Sailing Statues

Testimony from resident of Winchester Bay, Oregon who wishes to remain anonymous

Location Notes: There used to be a lighthouse here back in the day—well, it's still here, but there's no more electricity running to it, and the sea has risen halfway up to the gallery deck (colorfully called the "widow's walk"). Locals do their best to keep a fire going up top, tending the flame by rowing up to the lighthouse and climbing a ladder installed on the side—when they have the energy to do so (see statement below).

Despite the chill we've all assembled at the shore, sniffing the breeze for hints of spring, looking out toward the sea and waiting for our next statue to arrive. We can never be certain which day it will come, but after all these years, we've come to expect it during the first week of May, and befitting the season, it is a generally happy time, even if the message we receive some years is less than pleasant.

There have been years when we've waited, naked and shivering, hoping that year's statue would be clothed. There are years when we all cheer upon sighting the marble likeness of a well-dressed, prosperous merchant, or the silver statue of a queen, auguring good fortune for the entire town. And indeed, those years have been bountiful for everyone, sheep's wool growing thick and soft, chickens sitting high on stacks of eggs, cows producing more and sweeter milk than ever before.

Likewise, we wail on the years when a statue of a penniless urchin or a haggard old crone hobbles on undulating waves toward our shore.

Our auguries arrive on rafts barely large enough to hold them, plying in from the sea on the power of sails scarcely bigger than bedsheets. The wood is like nothing that grows around here, slim trunks lashed together with rough, dark coir. We've learned to let the rafts complete their journeys until they're beached, because the year we tried to assist the splintered oak Madonna to shore, we almost lost her to the waves. Many wish we had, for our year of hairshirts and piety was a long one.

Still, no one questions our seers' interpretations, no matter how onerous the burden, because the statues bring good fortune to our shores more often than not. Good will blossomed the year we received a pair of gargoyles: families grew closer, friendships deepened, and the whole community flourished. Many years we are blessed with likenesses of Poseidon, with his extraordinary bounty. We are all happy to participate in the mending of nets and the salting and drying of fish.

This year as always, we kept our ears pricked for the call, for our watchers at the shore to sound the bell when they spotted this year's statue. It was a bright windy day when we heard it, and we all raced to the sea, shielding our eyes from the glare with our hands. We began guessing as waves tossed the raft ever closer to land.

It's some sort of beast.

A camel?

An elephant?

Is it a bear?

We could barely look at it for the gleam of the sun on its burnished metal surface, reflecting an odd rosy hue.

The object bore no resemblance to anything we'd ever seen before: some sort of animal fitted together from bulbous, elongated sections of metal, polished to a high, shining pink. Its ears and tail stood erect, almost as long as its four legs. Its nose poked forward, ending in a simple knot.

That day, when the tiny raft sloughed onto sand, no one rushed to retrieve the statue. The chief seer approached it, under weight of duty, her reluctance to touch it evident. She ran a hesitant palm along its side, pronouncing it *warm, smooth, shining, bulging, though*—she knocked—*empty. Hollowed out, but still standing, still proud and erect, like our nation.*

Had we not cheered so lustily at that point, things might have ended differently.

Pink, not a full-blooded red, she then added.

We murmured, a few residual giggles floating over the crowd.

Not red, she said. *Not full of blood.*

We cheered again, our thoughts on spring flowers and pink youthful blushes and warm sun, the absence of blood presaging peace and life.

The chief seer raised her hand to quiet us. *We will be proud and stand tall like this beast. We will shine like this beast. We will empty ourselves of blood like this beast.*

She no longer needed a hand to quiet us.

Seer, countered an elder, *surely a statue this beautiful could not augur death.*

Of course not, she replied. *As you see, the beast still stands. It has been purified.*

The bloodlettings began the following day.

The spring drained away into a hot, languorous summer. Farmers had only enough strength to tend half their crops. Overfull cows bellowed in the fields when their milkmaids fainted away. Fishermen only dared to use their smallest nets, lest the weight be too much to haul back to shore.

The seers maintain that this is all necessary, to cleanse our bodies and spirits. We have been fortunate for too many years; this is required to maintain balance. The seers take part too, even the chief seer, with the exception of three who retain enough strength to manage the process properly. These three have tasked themselves with ensuring that our treasures remain safe, that our jewels are polished, our silver still shining, our finest garments still soft, our food still rich and flavorful, all of it befitting the celebration we will enjoy when the year of bleeding is over.

Month after month, we have returned to sit by the waves for our bleedings, watching the chief seer, waiting for her to tell us when it would be enough. At some point, she closed her eyes. They remain closed.

Now we all lie on the sand under the watchful eye of our well-fed minders, our heads turned toward the sea, yearning, praying for the next statue to arrive.

FROM: Meena Gupta
TO: Manfred Himmelblau
CC: Joseph Evans

Subject: In the City of Fretting Books, Crescent City, California

Transcript of Interview with Emily Arbuckle (EA), Mayor (and, seemingly, only human inhabitant)

Location Notes: This city is also not what it once was. The airport is long gone, submerged along with the beaches, homes, shops, and Ocean World—in fact, the whole place is an ocean world right up to the edge of the redwood forest, its trees bleached and spindly from salinization at the edges. The books flap and fret amongst the remaining healthy redwoods deeper into the forest.

EA: You won't be able to hear them now; they don't speak to strangers. They'll let themselves be rifled through, half hoping to be bought, remaining utterly still and silent to avoid upsetting a potential customer. They're remainders, you see. And once they became sentient, we didn't feel it was right to pulp them. So, they came here, out to pasture one might say—but in this case the pasture is a forest.

Since you won't be able to hear them firsthand, I took the liberty of making some videos so you can see them in action, at least secondhand.

VIDEO: [dry, whispery murmurs] *Am I entertaining enough? Will I captivate readers? Do I have what it takes?*

MG: What's that flapping sound?

AG: That's the books churning, flipping their pages with a critical eye.

VIDEO: *Is this chapter too big? Does this cover make me look fat?*

MG: And what are they doing now. Are they reading each other?

AG: Reading and writing. You see, the books write and rewrite themselves, endlessly opening one another to check their facts, to ensure their dates are correct—even the fiction books want to be convincing, after all. Regardless of genre, they ruffle about, rehearsing dialogues then scratching them out of existence, interrogating their narrative arcs, doubting their own timelines. Like this one…

VIDEO: *Could it really have happened that way? And even if it did, should it have? Wouldn't things have been more exciting/just/logical/compelling if something altogether different had happened instead?*

MG: So, with all of this self-editing, are any of these books even the ones they started out as?

EA: It's hard to say. The books write and rewrite themselves so many times it all becomes meaningless. They readjust their realities to the extent that nothing has really happened, and nothing else can hew to, or deviate from, the truth.

Let me fast forward a little here. I want to show you…

Here we are. See here? The poetry chapbooks look on the whole kerfuffle with an amused eye. They slip past one another, wondering how it came to be that they occupied this part of the forest while the prose books kept separate quarters. But their thoughts are often occupied with other matters. They have much to discuss amongst themselves: admiring each other's covers and contemplating each other's content before adding poems to their own pages, clearly marked "in conversation with..."

Every once in a while the chapbooks wish there weren't quite so many of them around, with new arrivals every day. Understandable, but they still don't like to admit it. They hold their (metaphorical) heads up and smile, not wanting to cause a fuss. Perhaps just a quick comment about trends, or a vague comment about a certain kind of chapbook today, or a reference to how another sort of chapbook might have been more... more.

Oh, here's a good bit:

VIDEO: *Still, in the end, let the prose books write and rewrite themselves, recombining their pages, cracking their overlarge spines in tussles over shelf space. We chaps will glide on in our own private corners, sharing space, in conversation, illuminating the adventurous and contemplative traveler, anointing them with light that they see only once they've arrived.*

[END REPORT.]

[Note: Due to persisting earthquake damage and sea level rise, we won't be able to continue along the coast to visit The City of Blooming Beasts. We'll have to head inland and continue our reporting from safer terrain.]

[Second note: Thanks for your email, Manfred. Yes, I'm aware that we're not here to speculate on the "who" or the "how" of the...changes. And I'm sure the "why" is out of the question. But can we get a little more clarification on the "what" that was being tested in the first place?]

V.

It's my favorite time of day: night. The moon is full, casting its silvery light over the desert. Shadows stretch, undulating with the dunes in front of us. I unwind the shawl from around my head to shake out the sand, and wipe grit from around my neck for what feels like the millionth time. I'm looking for a spot to sit for a quick rest when I see what looks like the roof of a house sticking up over the next dune.

"Is there a town here?" I ask, peering ahead into darkness.

Mama shakes her head. "Wasn't supposed to be one."

"Maybe there is," I say, picking up my pace. "I could go for a shower. Maybe there's a restaurant. Do we have enough for a—"

That's when I trip into a divot in the sand.

Mama helps me up and examines the ground while I shake out my shawl again. "Careful," she cautions. "Terrain's really uneven here."

I look around and, sure enough, I see furrows slashed into the sand. The lion and serpent have caught up to us by now, and we pick our way between the creases, which are long and straight, and intersect roughly at right angles.

The dune begins to slope downward now, revealing the remnants of a neighborhood. The rooftop I spotted is the top of a two-story house, the ground floor half-buried.

"Abandoned?" I ask.

"Seems to be," Mama says. "Probably pretty well picked over, but you never know..."

It wasn't always like that. When the fences first started sneaking, people stayed up at night, shotguns on their laps, staring down property lines. But eventually they had to sleep. They grew used to awaking to a brand new world, like the time Mama López opened her eyes to a fence around her bed. Her grandchildren slipped her a book and a thermos of tea, and the fence snuck away while she napped.

Yes, some people took liberties at first: teenagers took "their" new cars out for joyrides, but the rearranged map didn't let them get very far, streets closed off by roadblocks funneling them right back to where they'd started. When thieves tried to flee with newfound riches, they found themselves walled off from escape—then, overnight, from the riches.

And so they grew to trust the fences, despite their sneaking ways. Because, as they used to say: "When what was yours yesterday is mine today, and what's mine today is everyone's tomorrow, what are fences—and the things they fence—really for?"

After the lion finishes his story, it seems quiet until the clamor of shifting fences catches my attention again. Outside, stones fly through the air, stacking themselves into a wall around the roof of a rusted-out car.

"So what happened?" asks the serpent. "Where did they all go?"

The lion shrugs. "I guess trust didn't work in the long run." He looks at me and Mama, who leans against the wall with her arms crossed.

When we hear the thump of a foot on the stairs, we all move closer together. Mama turns off the lamp and clutches her spear while I unsheath my knife. I hold my breath to hear better: heavy footsteps, probably boots, two sets. Whispering. My heart pounds as the steps come closer.

"Hello, Miss." It's a deep voice, a man's. "We saw you up here through the window; thought we'd see who came to visit." His voice is honeyed, cloying. Poisonous. They must have seen me when I looked out the window. Followed me up here. That's never a good thing on the road.

Mama steps in front of me. "We don't want any trouble. We'll be on our way."

"Oh, there's two of 'em," says the other voice, chuckling. "Lucky us."

This is one of many times I've wished we had more than a spear and a knife to our name.

When two figures appear in the gloom at the top of the stairs, the serpent rears up with a hiss and the lion bares his teeth in a low, rumbling growl. The figures at the doorway stop cold.

"There are more than two of us here," says the lion, padding toward the men. He lets out a roar that vibrates in my chest and sends them stumbling down the stairs. I hear shouting and knocking around downstairs and look out the window just in time to see them running away, ducking bricks and fenceposts as they go.

Mama snatches me away from the window. "Sit down; that's what brought them up here in the first place."

I want to ask her, *Really, it's my fault men are evil?* But I don't argue. I slide my knife back into its sheath and sit—I don't want her to see that I'm shaking.

Mama clears her throat. "Thank you, Cat, Serpent."

"Thank you," I say. I know I sound more angry than grateful, which doesn't make sense because they're not the ones I'm mad at. But they're the only ones around to be mad at. I hate being on the road, always looking over our shoulders. Will we ever find anywhere we can be safe?

I sit with my knees up, arms crossed over them, and listen to the metallic shiver of flying fences.

story: she was playing by herself, no one was with her, undermining our theory that the trees' bullet had grazed her on its way toward another intended target. But her story never changed, and she professed not to have the slightest idea what might have prompted the trees to take aim at—or near—her.

Mia insisted she'd gone outside because she woke up from a bad dream, and she was too hot and it was too quiet and she thought she heard a bird outside her window and didn't want to think about the bad dream anymore, so she went out to see if she could find the bird. And when asked what the dream was about, she would simply say she didn't remember, which could mean either she didn't remember it when she woke up, or the *thwwp* of the bullet through her pigtail whooshed any memory of the dream completely out of her head.

Many of us thought everyone should just lay off poor Mia, who certainly didn't ask to be the recipient of a near miss on her way home. We worried she could well be (re)traumatized with all the questioning. Others—including her own mother mind you—disagreed, wanting to get to the bottom of this incident. Was it intentional, or a first and only misfire? A fluke or a foretaste? A warning? And if so, what should Mia do, or not do, to protect herself? Or was it a case of the sins of the father (or mother) being visited upon the son (or in this case, daughter)?

Should her father be spending more time with her (he did miss her last two recitals at school)? Or should her mother not have complained to the principal when Mia's teacher commented on her chubby cheeks? She didn't want her daughter developing a complex over her weight, but she also hadn't intended for the teacher to get a reprimand. And soon enough, something about the mountain hemlock in her backyard, the way its limbs swayed in the breeze, began to suggest to Mia's mother that trees weren't very fond of people who stirred the pot, even a little, even for a good reason. They just might have given her daughter a near miss as a warning to her, the mother herself, not to be so eager to snitch on others in the future.

So when she heard the rumor that this same teacher had had the audacity to joke about being next on the arboreal hit list for "ruffling parental feathers," Mia's mother waited for the trees to act. And she waited. And waited. Until she decided that she still had no idea why they had targeted little Mia for a near miss, and whether they would strike again. And because Mia's mother couldn't move her family away—because none of us are allowed to move—she's simply stopped going outside, and has forbidden the whole family from doing so as well, because who knows what the trees will do next?

Now, for most of us, that way of thinking is a bit extreme. The trees only take a couple of us a year, and normally for reasons that are, if not completely proportional, at least somewhat clear. And with such a small number from a large population, compared to national averages, we're actually rather safe. So even if we wanted to leave, and even if we could, how would we fare out there? Certainly no worse, and certainly not enough to risk the brunt of the trees' excellent marksmanship. Guests can come and go as they please, even after an extended stay—with the caveat that the trees ultimately decide how long a "visit" actually lasts. And it's not like we receive many guests, because why would you visit a city whose main feature is something you hope to never experience firsthand?

Still, it has become a phenomenon among young travelers, primarily male, to approach a visit here as a running of the bulls scenario. They'll come and place themselves in temporal danger, drinking and lounging, all the while feeling out the situation for a hint of when a visit becomes a sojourn. Most of them play it safe, never engaging lodgings for more than a week at a time, but one bold soul extended his stay for a month, and at the end of that period, found it impossible to leave. Gunfire rang out the first morning he walked with his backpack toward the bus station, bullets lodging themselves in the dirt inches from his toes. The unfortunate driver he hired that afternoon as an alternative wound up having to repair her bullet-ridden vehicle. If this guest went anywhere with his backpack or made any movement toward a bus or a car, or even wandered too close to the edge of the city, bullets erupted from the forest. That was ten years ago. He's since settled down, gotten married (he was quite the catch, a rare new arrival who stayed) and has a house and two children of his own now.

It's not a terrible life. The trees protect us and ask little in return. We make sure they have enough water, spray for pests, pull down parasitic vines before they establish their chokeholds. The trees themselves have eradicated all the woodpeckers and beavers, bullet by bullet. We all get along quite happily until the trees decide we've done something wrong. And if we can never quite predict what that will be, never know when our number will be up, well, how different is that really from anywhere else?

FROM: Meena Gupta
TO: Manfred Himmelblau
CC: Joseph Evans

Subject: In the City of Bingeing Bats

Transcription of notes scrawled in splotchy black ink on scraps of charred paper near Mineral, California. Due to the condition of the notes, it is difficult to say with certainty if we've reassembled them correctly.

Location Notes: I know this isn't scientific, but can I say how much of a relief it is to be up in the mountains? These aren't even the tall ones yet, and it's already so much cooler. We keep seeing these vintage signs around with snowshoes and skis on them—you can imagine what it was like when they used to get snow. The old "eco-friendly" vehicle charging stations are still around the National Park area, signs that they were trying.

We used to eat the obvious fare.[1] At dusk we flooded out from our barns and belfries and attics, squealing for the coordinates of our next meal. We spent most of the night swooping and scooping our sustenance, one tiny insect at a time.

During the day, if we couldn't sleep, we listened to the shows the humans watched in their rooms below us.[2] Our ears perked up at the stories about bats from different parts of the world. We learned about fruit bats and thought they sounded exotic.[3] Maybe we'd try some fruit on our next vacation, we said. Then one of us said "Why wait?" and the rest of us said, "Why, indeed?"

So next sundown we flew until we located an orchard, and while the Granny Smiths were a bit tart for our tastes, the peaches were a revelation. We denuded the peach trees and fluttered back home to sleep, juice still dripping up our faces onto the floor.

The following night, to our dismay, there were no more peaches.

"What a crock," we screeched. "How do those fruit bats survive?"

[1] Moths, mosquitoes, beetles, gnats, and so on.

[2] Our favorite shows were game shows and true crime, perhaps because they told us so much about you.

[3] For the record, many of us were uncomfortable with the use of the word "exotic," but bats tend not to bicker unless it's about food, mates, or room to roost.

And on and on until one of us said, "They're not just peach bats, idiots; they're fruit bats."

"Oh yeah," we said, and we went off in search of other kinds of fruit.

One evening we gorged on blackberries. Another night we demolished a whole strawberry patch. We developed a taste for the sweetest varieties: cherries, raspberries, red grapes, and plums. When we cleaned out a whole tree of mulberries before they were fully ripe, we realized it wasn't the sweetness we were after—it was the color. Anything red piqued our interest.

We expanded our palates to tomatoes, bell peppers, rhubarb, and red cabbages. One night when we happened upon the bounty of a split watermelon, our minds and menu expanded by a whole patch of melons. Still, bit by bit, we ran out of red upon which to feed.

You see where this is going.[4]

Yes, we admit, our colony became quite the cliché, stealing into pastures at night and draining whole herds of cattle dry. We

[4] *Or wait, maybe you don't see quite yet where this is going, because most of you humans think bats are completely blind. In fact, we can imagine some of you raising your hands right now to ask how we can tell which fruits are red, ready to gently suggest that the writer of this story should look up some facts about bat perception, that she would find the part about echolocation especially interesting. And rest assured she did, but she also found the part about how some bats can actually see color to be quite interesting as well. Or perhaps the author already knows this because she is herself a bat. In fact, she's probably exasperated at the assumption that she can't see, and likely rankles at that expression, "blind as a—" You know the one...*

weren't particularly helpful in terms of uplifting the species.

We know, we know, bats like us are part of the problem. But have you ever whiled away an hour on a cow's back, just out of tail's reach, sipping at the tiny well your teeth have gouged into its skin, that salty warm liquid rising to meet your tongue as you lap lap lap it in? We know what you think of us,[5] and although we're not supposed to say this in polite society, there is a kernel of truth to most stereotypes. But by now, who are we trying to be nice for?

Seriously, who? We sucked this city's last human family dry months ago. We wish we'd have been able to get more of them before they fled, but there you have it. To tell you the truth, as much as we loved to binge on their blood, they were also massive pains in our asses. Even before all of their livestock were gone, they started coming after us, setting out traps and poisons, smoking us out of our attics.[6]

After one dimwit burned down a belfry trying to chase us out, a

[5] We know what you call groups of us: camp, colony, cloud, even cauldron. A cauldron of bats. Not something you'd bring home to mother.

[6] Not that we would wish contagion upon ourselves, but it surprised us that nobody thought to infect us with white-nose fungus, our greatest foe. That tells you the level of human intellect we were dealing with.

whole procession of fools with jittery torches marched through the streets to chase us out of town. Nothing that happened that evening was truly our fault.

Some of us relocated to the caves on the outskirts; others stayed and drained every person they laid claws on. Only a few humans escaped, yelling things like "help" and "containment" and "extermination."[7]

By now you've tried aerial poisons, burnings, have even contemplated drone attacks, although you'd have to carpet-bomb the city to truly get rid of us.[8] Maybe you're still considering the people who used to own the structures. But we own them now.

You may wonder how we still survive, having sucked the blood out of everything for miles, without—as far as you can tell—having begun to dine on each other.

We bats are resourceful. We work together. While half of us keep our homes safely occupied, the rest go out and binge. When we come home, we feed each other. [9]

[7] *Those exterminators were tasty, by the way. Thanks for sending them out.*

[8] *Funny how you're squeamish about doing this in some places of the world, but not others— remember, we used to listen to your news reports.*

[9] *Those who can, provide milk; others feed their comrades mouth to mouth, regurgitating sweetness, filling them up with the richness of their excess.*

And although we must fly long distances,[10] we find plenty to eat. We can feed on anything by now. We've perfected the art of soundless flight, the delicate descent onto a sleeping creature, the soft nip of skin and silent lap of blood. We've learned to drink until we can barely fly, and can lift off without waking our hosts.

Only on occasion, if we've drunk more than we should have, might a creature sense a shift in weight and startle awake as we take flight. And perhaps you would understand us better if you could feel this too, this uncanny intimate distance, suspended in air above an animal whose blood still warms your tongue, watching the creature flick its tail, or scramble upright with a snort, or fumble for the bedside lamp gasping:

[10] *Did you know that some species of bat have been known to migrate over 1,000 miles?*

Do you wonder if we're one of those species?

You should.

What was that?

FROM: Meena Gupta
TO: Manfred Himmelblau

Subject: A little guidance

You'll be happy to hear that Joseph has been quite disciplined in his adherence to the strict "observation only" protocol. Frustratingly so. Even in private conversation. I was hoping you might reassure him that informal speculation as to the intended purpose of these alchemical experiments—not who, mind you, but what they were hoping to achieve—doesn't constitute an official statement, and will not be recorded, and may actually help us become more astute observers.

At first I thought the changes were about neutralizing dangers (the knives and perhaps the fences), but most of them seem to have created new ones (trees, bats, even statues). Was this by design?

Again, I'm not asking which branch of the "who" we're not supposed to be talking about might have been behind this, but—what exactly was the desired goal? It just all seems so random to me.

FROM: Manfred Himmelblau
TO: Meena Gupta

Subject: Patience

My dearest Meena, the very inquisitiveness that causes you such frustration in the moment will be useful later in your career—but I must emphasize the word *later*. I look forward to our debrief when your observation trip is completed.

VI.

The sun beats down on us, ever higher, ever hotter, each hour shrinking our four shadows on the sand: mother, daughter, M and me. We've been traveling for days, taking what little shelter we can find under spindly acacias to rest during the hottest hours, walking through the night. We've been fortunate to travel under the light of a full moon, but it's waning bit by bit, as is our water—I learned how to open the flask by watching the humans.

The woman silently points her spear—not a lightning stick, it turns out—toward an outcropping of stone that casts the only shadow for miles, and we march toward it. The farther north we travel, the more moisture the ground holds. When we stop, the humans sip from their single canteen while M and I scratch away the topmost layer of dust and lie down, stretching out against the soil to absorb trace amounts of moisture. In this small way, I sense progress. Desperation loses its edge with even the tiniest bit of water.

I take a closer look at the humans, who still seem gangly and awkward from this angle. The mother's hair is dark and cropped close to her head. The daughter's wavy hair is pulled back in a ponytail. They both have brown skin, but the daughter's is a bit lighter than her mother's, and her eyes are hazel, whereas the mother's are brown. These differences are puzzling to me, because as I understand it, children come directly out of mothers. But then again, M and I have slight variations in color as well, despite being cut from the same stone.

The mother constantly places herself between her daughter and us, keeping a distance, which is fine with me. If they could hurt us, they probably would have by now, but I still feel vulnerable so close to them. And yet, we need them. Those birds that reassured me early in our journey haven't reappeared. Only the humans seem to have a plan.

M shimmies to reach more moisture. His head lolls in the humans' direction. "Why didn't you tell us we were this close?" he asks.

The woman frowns. "What, Cat?"

She never calls us by our names even though I introduced us. The daughter told us their names too: Rose. Dolores. The round "o" sounds echo inside my mouth like the church choir on Sundays, before they all left and everything crumbled. It's a pleasant feeling, but I'm not sure if we should be using their names if they're not using ours. I'm not clear on the rules.

"Don't you hear that?" M asks. He looks at me and I shake my head.

The girl's eyes widen. "You hear Carson City already?"

"There's *something* up ahead. Music."

We all look in the direction M nods, seeing nothing.

The woman's frown deepens. "I didn't think we were that close. We should wait a little longer, though. The heat." But she closes the bag of nuts she and the girl have been eating from, as though we're leaving right now. We're all concerned about our dwindling water supply.

Well, all of us except M. But I don't want to think about our backup—I wish I hadn't told him my idea. I rise and scratch out a new divot to lie down in.

Time crawls; the few shadows offered by the stony outcropping lengthen slowly. Even though it's still hot, we can't wait any longer.

M and I rise and shake ourselves off. The humans take one last sip of water before we resume our northward journey. M leads, tilting his head this way and that as we walk. The woman is skeptical, but admits his path is in the same general direction we were heading, so we keep on trudging, all of us silent, M and I in front, the humans at a distance behind us.

Then I hear it. It's a song but not a song, a hint of something on a breeze that's not blowing.

"You hear it now," says M.

I nod. "But…"

"It's like when we used to have winter storms, when wind whipped through the trees around the church."

Yes, that's part of it, something whistling through naked branches. But there's something more: "Are those voices?" I look back to make sure it's not the woman and her daughter talking. "I hear human voices."

M squints to concentrate. "Moaning. And not the pleasurable kind—which, mind you, I only know because I heard both kinds in that supposedly holy building." He grunts. "Hypocrites."

Whatever he thinks of humans, the bad sort of moaning is a reason for concern. I stop and wait until the rest of our party reaches us.

"What?" asks the woman.

"You don't hear that?"

They both listen for a moment before shaking their heads.

I'm about to warn them when M turns and continues walking toward the noise. I tell him to wait and he does, begrudgingly.

"You don't hear that wind?" I insist.

"Wind? I wish," the woman says. "We'd better keep going. Sun's getting low, and I want to get there before the merchants close up shop for the evening."

It seems early, but she's right: the sky is just beginning to take on the golden burnish of sunset. There's no way it should be this late in the afternoon already, but I shake off my unease and join the rest of the group, which is already moving on.

With each step the sun seems to sink lower, and the wind grows louder, although I don't feel so much as a breeze. The humans gradually

A choir burns from this new bonfire, soft and angelic, singing words I don't understand, voices soaring in some ancient melody, echoing like we're in a big empty room. I look up into the night sky to check that we're still outside. Sparks from the bonfire meander overhead.

Mama prods me, and I wonder how long I've been staring up into the air. The two creatures are gazing into the flames, and I don't know why, but I feel sad for them. They look like they've lost something. Or maybe they're what's lost. Or we all are.

I realize then it's the eyes—the reason I think I can trust the serpent. Even though it looks like a snake, its eyes are more like ours, roundish with a circular pupil. The lion's pupils are mean-looking slits like a snake's. Both creatures seem all mixed up, purposely designed to make people uncomfortable.

The serpent notices me watching them and nudges the lion.

We keep moving.

The next bonfire has a looping, burbling melody, rising and falling like a river singing. It's so quiet I can hear the popping of wood underneath. The one after that buzzes like a million bees, their pitch spiking randomly up and down.

Every once in a while I remember to look around, chiding myself for getting sloppy. We haven't seen anyone—or anything—but that doesn't mean there's no danger lurking in the dark. Still, when I get to the next fire it's hard to imagine anything bad could happen to us surrounded by this new, soothing flutter. I close my eyes and imagine hummingbirds.

The lion growls, but I don't feel like walking anymore. I don't even want to open my eyes. I just want to stand here a little longer in the cool night air scented with wood smoke, stretching my palms out toward the heat of the flames, listening to these hummingbirds and butterflies. I can almost feel wings tickling my cheeks, my nose.

The lion roars.

I open my eyes, blink myself back to attention. Mama's rubbing her hands over her face, then she tips her head back and rolls it to the front like she's just woken up. With a start, she picks up the spear she's let fall to the ground.

The two creatures stand expectantly up ahead, silhouetted by flickers of orange and yellow.

"This is the last one," calls out the serpent.

Mama turns away from the hummingbird fire and shuffles forward. It's like walking through quicksand to follow her. Something strange is going on here—but does that mean we have to leave?

I don't want to lose sight of Mama so I keep moving, one sluggish step after another. A quiet sobbing comes from the bonfire up ahead. Mama shakes her head and veers off to the right, and I don't blame her, because although the weeping isn't loud, it's heart-wrenching. The bonfire's crying burrows into me, like worms tunneling down through my ears into my whole body, laying down sticky trails of sadness.

I follow Mama away from the sobbing bonfire, but I can still hear it when yet another bonfire comes into view—and earshot. This one is also a pit of misery, whimpering and moaning. The smoke thickens.

"You said that was the last one," I complain.

"We thought it was." The serpent's voice startles me, so close—I hadn't kept track of where he was.

Mama changes course again, heading away from the new fire as its whimpering grows into full-on wailing. I hunch with my hands over my ears and move forward, but it's almost like the noise is following us. I quicken my pace to a jog, but I'm too exhausted to keep it up for more than a few paces. Ahead, Mama staggers and drops to a knee, head bowed.

Another fire burns ahead of us. It's also wailing.

When I reach Mama, she's kneeling, curled into herself with her hands over her ears. I drop to my knees, wanting to put my arms around her, but I can't bear to unstop my ears either. The wailing and screeching presses against my hands like it's battering for entry, and all I can do is hunch next to her, press myself against her. I cough, smoke burning my throat, and shut my stinging eyes. A spasm of coughing curls me even tighter into myself, until my forehead touches the ground. The dirt is rough but cool against my burning skin…

FROM: Joseph Evans
TO: Manfred Himmelblau
CC: Meena Gupta

Subject: In the City of Floating Wolves

Transcription of notes in a pocket-sized field journal found on the eastern edge of Plumas National Forest, California (physical journal to be sent via post)

Location Notes: Technically we're still in Plumas National Forest, but to be clear, this is no forest. It is a graveyard of trees. Drought, fungus, beetles, and fires have reduced the eastern edge of the forest to a smattering of scabby trunks on a slope of sand. The desert reaches its vast, dusty hand ever westward.

The window is still open. The window is always open, and there are always drops of blood on the windowsill, always stray bits of viscera on the floor. Always all that's left of the body. A leaf or a tuft of fur confirms what everyone has come to expect: wolves. It doesn't matter what floor one is on—for example, the top floor—or how fine the home—for example, the mayor's house. The wolves always get in.

He should have known better than anyone not to open the window. He was the one who hired you to come do something about the wolves.

The sheriff shakes his head and mutters, *It was bound to catch up with him.*

What? you ask.

Everything, he says, using tweezers to transfer a strand of coarse grey hair from the windowsill to a baggie. To confirm what everyone knows.

# # #

You never expected this. When you answered the mayor's letter, and he wrote back, repeating the word "floating," you thought it was merely figurative. You thought it meant the wolves were happy, and of course you had your doubts, which is why you felt it was so important that you go.

All those months ago, when that scratchy, long-distance phone call came in from a land line in Quincy, California, you googled while the mayor spoke of floating wolves. After only ten minutes of talking, he offered you an assignment to continue the work your research collaborator had begun (the details of which he hadn't shared with you). The mayor offered you a generous salary, and you searched in vain for any mention of floating wolves while wondering if they were offering you as much as your collaborator had been paid.

We'll pick you up from the airport, said the mayor.

You told yourself these "floating" wolves needed a protector. Surely they were only reacting to some perceived threat.

You went, just to see. You saw. You stayed.

# # #

You follow a trickle of blood past the bakery, the diner, the church festooned with leering marble gargoyles. You don't usually find these many traces, extending for this distance. The trail gradually dissipates into a drop of blood here, a bit of skin there, until those also dry up. You keep walking in the same direction, asking if anyone has seen anything. But even though there are no witnesses, no tracks, they all insist this is to be expected in the City of Floating Wolves.

Have you ever seen a pawprint here? ask the townsfolk.

You walk away from the aromas of bread and coffee, heading toward peat and moss, toward the flutter of cottonwood leaves and the prick of pine needles. You don't even care about finding this particular wolf (or *wolves?* Good god, after all this time you don't even know that much). Birds twitter and twigs crackle under your boots as you walk into the sun-speckled forest. The path curves to the right, and you almost follow it. Almost.

These wolves float.

You part the branches and step into the underbrush.

# # #

They've given you the notes your research collaborator left behind. His theory was the wolves don't come for just anyone. They don't come for the innocent, or those who think of themselves as such. They don't necessarily come for the wicked either—only for those who think of themselves that way. They come for the troubled, the beleaguered, the guilt-riddled. Sometimes the cause is obvious. At times the victim even leaves a note before sliding the window open to the night.

Early in your stay, you installed recording equipment inside the home of the man reported to be the evilest in town. There have been no wolves; but on the other hand, he has also not engaged in any behavior befitting his reputation.

Perhaps, for man and wolf alike, it is because they know they are being watched.

# # #

Twigs rake your face and vines tug at your boots as you struggle through the forest. You don't know what you're looking for, exactly, or how high you should look. Will there be a corpse in the crook of a tree? Do the wolves slink among the trunks at eye level, or float above the canopy?

You hadn't planned on entering the forest. You thought you'd just take notes and leave, but you couldn't resist the unusually strong trail of clues. You repeatedly feel for the bear spray on your utility belt, ensuring yourself it's still there. Your pistol sits uselessly at home.

With every step, you ask yourself why you're still out here, why you didn't ask for anyone to come with you. They would have laughed and shaken their heads, as they always do when you talk about going into the woods. But walking alone you allow yourself a bit of magical thinking: perhaps this time someone would have come.

But they didn't. And you're at risk, just as anyone might be. Certainly you're not blameless; far from it. Do you think your position will keep you safe? The mayor apparently thought so. Do you think your curiosity insulates you? Your virtue, the selfless researcher come to keep the wolves safe?

If there's anything you've found, it's that they're not the ones who need saving.

# # #

You've asked people why they stay. They look at you with wonder, pity, suspicion. They narrow their eyes and answer your question with a question: *Why do* you *stay?*

To study the wolves, you answer.

They nod. *That's why you came,* they say, *but why do you* stay?

At first you wondered whether the wrong things weren't being investigated, whether it was the people who needed a good examination. But then... then you began to wonder why *you do* stay. You've seen what the wolves do—not directly, but the aftermath—and there's no way to predict who they will visit next. When he was still alive, the mayor told you the pattern: it seemed a person only knew the wolves were coming on the evening they were to arrive. And by then, the wolves were welcomed.

At first you found it difficult to believe that someone would open their door or window to a wolf. But some nights, alone with your thoughts, your second and third guesses, you can imagine why it might seem like release.

# # #

You tromp through the forest, following the same direction as far as you can tell. Even though you're lifting your feet, wispy vines still snake up from the earth to snag your toes. It's the little things that get you.

No one blamed you outright, but you're doing enough of that on your own. All the sympathy for the loss of your colleague—your research collaborator of decades—slid right off your back like water off a wolf pelt. You both knew he was taking unnecessary risks. You could have intervened. But you wanted that prize as much as he did, so you didn't say a word.

Because you also wanted his wife.

When you stop, wishing for the hundredth time you'd brought water, it hits you: silence. No birdsong. No small creatures rustling about in the underbrush. You look up into the trees, squinting at the sun slanting through the trunks (is it possible you've been in the forest for that many hours?). No breeze fluttering the leaves. The forest has gone still.

Out of the corner of your eye you see a shadow passing smoothly between the trees. It disappears when you turn toward it. After a moment's hesitation you scramble to follow, heart thumping at your luck. Except it isn't luck, is it? Whatever you've been tracking has eluded you for hours, weeks, months. It wouldn't have allowed itself to be seen unless it wanted you to see it.

You stop.

# # #

Stop hovering, he'd said while packing his gear. *I'll be fine.*

At least tell me where you're going, you said.

But he didn't. He never quite trusted you, despite the partnership the two of you projected to the public. You couldn't exactly blame him. You told yourself it was the press' fault for focusing their attention on the female researcher, for putting you in the spotlight.

Only once he'd arrived at his destination did he call you. It was the same area code as where you are now.

Don't worry, I know what I'm doing, he told you before going out on what would become his last observation. You didn't believe in a wolf that would fail to defend its territory. But when you recall the glances you shared with his wife during his going-away dinner, pretending it was your first time in his home; how she so politely asked what kind of wine you prefer, as though you'd only met once before at a faculty function; how you insisted on helping her in the kitchen afterward, and he didn't have a problem in the world with letting the women clean up while he relaxed in the living room; how you ached to touch her again as you stood at her side, washing the same dish over and over; how, finally, you turned to face her, and your lips found hers while jazz spilled in through the closed kitchen door—it was then that you allowed yourself not to worry about him at all.

After his death, his contacts began searching for you. After all, they didn't know the truth behind your collaboration. He'd kept this project close to his chest after seeing how you'd insinuated yourself into the last one.

He was never very good at tracking multiple variables at once.

# # #

The slits of sunlight shining through the trees are fading. You could turn back now, tell people you never caught up with the wolves. You could fly back home and use your research collaborator's notes to publish articles respectfully summarizing his work, develop the studies into a book, which compassionate colleagues would read and assign to their classes. By now there has been a respectful interlude; you could check in on his wife, ask how she's faring, be seen commiserating, and let everyone witness how things take their natural course until you finally, bravely, clasp one another's hands, shaking your heads in amazement, *still grieving, but yes, very much in love,* insisting that *no one could have been more surprised* than the two of you.

But that wouldn't stop the wolves floating in your mind.

Another spot of darkness sweeps between the trunks farther ahead, and it almost seems inevitable that this night would come.

You follow.

FROM: Meena Gupta
TO: Manfred Himmelblau
CC: Joseph Evans

Subject: In the City of Crying Merchants

Traveling Researcher's Assessment of Carson City, Nevada

Location Notes: The relative wealth and success of this city are due to one thing and one thing only: Lake Tahoe. A mere twenty miles to the west, Lake Tahoe is the largest alpine lake in North America, and the second deepest in the West (only Oregon's Crater Lake is deeper). It still has two dozen tributaries feeding into it (down from over 60 a century ago), and its only outlet was into the Truckee River until the Tahoe Dam was permanently blocked off fifty years ago. Rebels from what used to be downriver (now downriverbed) keep Lake Security busy with their constant attempts to blow up the dam, which keeps the neighboring city of Carson City awash in commerce, providing food, housing, and supplies for both the rebels and the security forces. Despite all this, the city feels safe—I suppose both sides save their aggression for their scrimmages over the dam. At least, that's what I assume, because we couldn't really hear anyone over the crying. The recording was just as bad. So, with a decent transcript out of the question, my report is as follows:

This is a city I'll never understand.

Day and night there was wailing, only wailing, as morose merchants walked the streets tearing their shirts and beating their breasts.

After an initial survey of the area, we approached a flower merchant and asked what troubled him so.

"I have lost business to that man over there," he answered, pointing at another merchant across the street, who was also crying. When we went to see the other wares, we found they were completely different: the flower merchant was crying over sales lost to the fishmonger. He, in turn, was wailing over customers who'd crossed over to the candy seller, who mourned the customers leaving his stall to purchase books around the corner. Each merchant blamed the next, accusing them of unfair practices, cutthroat pricing, coercion, and defamatory gossip about the competition.

"How can you even compare a rose to a trout, or a bonbon to a book, or a loaf of bread to a packet of turmeric?" we asked. "Wouldn't it make sense to compare this baker to that one, or this florist to the other? Perhaps instead of crying you could ask yourselves what you could do to improve your own offerings."

By this time we were shouting to be heard over the din of their wailing and moaning. As soon as the last word left our mouths, however, the streets quieted. Men stopped poking their fingers at each other across the streets. They wiped their eyes and sniffled. For the first time since we'd entered the city, we felt relief—even hope.

Then an apple whooshed by my head. A newspaper thwacked Joseph's shoulder, and a stinking fish thwopped wetly against my back. After a stunned moment we ran, ducking heads of lettuce, wedges of cheese, pork chops, and bottles of perfume. We stopped at the end of the street, croissants and flowers bouncing off us as we turned to plead with the merchants.

"This is madness!" I yelled. "We only wanted to help, and now look, you've just driven out your very last customers!"

One last tomato squished on the ground, then all was quiet except for the flutter of loose pages and the trickle of milk running down the gutter. Then a sob.

"He threw the first sausage," moaned the spice merchant.

"Lies!" howled the butcher. He pointed a shaking finger at the ice cream peddler. "The first missile was a scoop of vanilla."

"Truly you are blind," the ice cream peddler responded. "Did you not see the cobbler throw the shoe?"

We turned and left the blubbering behind in the City of Crying Merchants.

FROM: Meena Gupta
TO: Manfred Himmelblau
RE: Patience

No questions this time. This is me practicing patience.

VIII.

I wake up on a lounge chair under a hazy blue sky. There's a fresh breeze and just enough cloud cover to make the sunlight pleasant rather than harsh. I rub my eyes, which are scratchy, just like my throat. My mouth is gritty and dry.

With a jolt I prop myself up on an elbow. Mama's awake too, on a lounge chair next to mine.

"Where are we?" I ask, looking around. I spot a couple of tall glasses of something on a small table between our lounges. I reach for one, parched, but Mama pushes her canteen into my hand instead. I shake it. It's almost empty, but she nods, so I drink. Of course it's not enough. I'm still woozy, still thirsty and hungry, and would love nothing more than some food and a nap. I lie back again, but Mama's sitting up, asking where her spear is, ready to go.

The gargoyles approach.

"You haven't touched them," says the serpent, gesturing at the glasses sweating condensation onto the table.

"You'll forgive me for not exactly trusting the source," Mama shoots back. "Where's my spear?"

The lion gives the serpent a look. Even on his carved face I can read derision.

"Don't worry, it's safe," says the serpent, nodding at the drinks. "We've had it ourselves. It's good."

"Where are we?" Mama demands to know. "What did you do with our weapons?"

"We're on a rooftop in—" The gargoyles exchange another glance before the serpent continues: "Our hosts have very generously provided refreshments, food and drink. It's all safe, they serve travelers all the time."

Mama's quiet now, with a wary expression. I smell the food, a faint luxurious aroma of bread and spices and warm, savory meats. But at the same time I hear something that makes my spine crawl—something low, guttural, growling.

This can't be. We've purposely been avoiding this place.

Mama stands, still wobbly, but angry. "You brought us to the City of Praying Devils?"

The serpent seems almost sorry. "They found us after we dragged you out of the bonfire field. You were hardly in any shape to go anywhere else."

I stand now too, to catch Mama if she falls.

"Just because we've spent most of our lives attached to one of your churches," the serpent says, "you shouldn't assume we're of the same mind regarding devils. Humans and devils have a notoriously bad history, but you shouldn't assume that's the only kind of relationship devils can have."

Mama crosses her arms. "Well, you all may be friendly with them, but we're leaving."

"We're not saying we're friends," the serpent hastens to explain. "It's more—neutral. We don't interfere with them; they don't interfere with us."

"Besides," says the lion, "they wouldn't harm paying customers."

"Who pa—" Mama pats her chest for her money pouch and opens it. "Where are our packs?"

"Right over there," he says, nodding behind us. And there they are, propped up against the wall.

Fuming, Mama rummages through her money pouch, taking stock. I told her we should split our funds more evenly, but she only lets me carry a little bit. Says that will keep me out of danger, keep the target off my back. But I don't see how.

"The prices are very reasonable here," the serpent reassures her.

I sense Mama calming as she closes her pouch again. They could have taken everything. Apparently, they didn't take very much at all.

Not to mention, they could have left us for dead.

"Drink," says the serpent, more invitation than command.

I purposely don't look at Mama as I pick up my glass and drink, closing my eyes at the balm of liquid coursing down my throat. If I die now, it'll be with the delicious taste of cinnamon lemonade on my tongue.

But I don't die, and now my stomach is alive and gurgling.

"Sounds like you're ready for a meal." The serpent—E—beckons us to follow him toward a long table heaped with food. The table is set up against a railing overlooking a courtyard. Even as saliva floods my mouth, I'm unnerved by the growling floating up to the rooftop from below. At least there aren't any devils up here with us—yet?

I'm powerless against the call of the buffet table crowded with steaming silver chafing dishes, platters heaped with vegetables and topped toasts and pastry puffs, bowls of fruit salads and potato salads and macaroni salads and bean salads and any kind of salads you could imagine. I dispense with all the manners Mama's taught me and nibble straight from the platters while loading a plate with cubes of cheese, cuts of beef, a chicken leg, a roll, mashed potatoes—

"Slow down girl," she mutters into my ear.

I can't help myself. It's been forever since I've seen so much food in one place. I stuff a mini pig-in-a-blanket into my mouth and close my eyes in bliss. Only once my mouth is properly full does my attention shift back to the noises drifting up from below. I lean over the railing as far as I dare.

Down on the ground, in a courtyard lined with box hedges and trellised, ivied walls, are devils as far as the eye can see. They're not all red, as I'd imagined they would be. Some are purple, or blue, or green. Many are part animal, covered in shaggy fur or sleek pelts. Some are smooth-skinned, and others are scaly, and still others are covered in something that shimmers like velour.

Most of the devils are bowing or walking in circles around neatly trimmed trees, palms upturned, faces tilted back in supplication. Some of them are crouching around a splashing fountain, and it's hard to tell if they're on hands and knees in worship or if they're simply comfortable on all fours. Some rock back and forth, some are still, and some crawl between the others like ants through blades of grass. Their eerie prayers rise up from below, a guttural murmur of hisses and clicks.

I watch them while stuffing another bite of cheese into my mouth. With all those devils, I expected it to be hot and smell like sulfur, but it's actually pleasant. I close my eyes and breathe in. The air is slightly humid, but there's a cool breeze up here carrying the scent of flowers. Magnolias?

I turn to the gargoyles. "Thank you for saving us, E and M."

E shows a lot of teeth, which I choose to assume is a smile. "Greetings."

I startle at a deep voice behind me and turn to find a man in a sharp, dark grey, pin-striped suit. His curly black hair shines, pouffy on top, sides cut short.

"Welcome to the City of Praying Devils. I am Askar, your host." His voice is as sweet and smooth as the honey I've slathered on my roll, which makes me want to take another bite, but that feels rude during an introduction. As he comes closer, I see the horns at his temples— he's cleverly hidden them in his hair, which I suppose is meant to make us feel more comfortable. Or trick us.

Mama places herself between us, but I lean a bit to see him better. When he smiles and asks if we have any questions, I notice a certain sharpness to his cheekbones, a piercing quality to his eyes. His upturned nose reminds me of a bat.

I step out from behind Mama and ask what the devils are praying for. "Oh, everything, really. Each one has different troubles and hopes. But let me see what I can pick up on at the moment." He cocks his head and closes his eyes in an attitude of listening. "Some are praying for more power, others for more riches. One wishes to couple with another. Yet another one is praying about a sick child."

"They're praying to heal a child?" Mama asks, skeptical.

"No. They're praying for the child to die. This *is* a city of devils."

I stiffen.

"I assure you," Askar says, "we have no interest in your demise. You are our guests." He smiles at each of us. "My gargoyle friends, where are your plates? Is the food not to your liking?"

E says, "We only need water, and we'd be grateful for more."

Our host calls out in a gurgling mutter. Some sort of gremlin-being scurries out to pour more water into cut crystal bowls set on lacquered trays close to the ground. M pads away for another drink, but E asks our host about Carson City

"Ah, yes, the City of Crying Merchants," he says. "That's a few days' journey from here. Keep going to the north. You'll hear it before you see it."

Mama nods, and I can tell she's annoyed. She thinks asking questions is the best way to reveal your ignorance. The way I see it, though, it's the only way to find out what you don't know, so I go ahead and ask how old The City of Praying Devils is.

"Ah," says Askar with a smile. "We have been here for centuries— you just weren't able to see us until the Testing."

I step over to the railing and look down at all the muttering, shifting, genuflecting devils below. "They've always been there?"

"They've always been everywhere," says the serpent. "Humans normally can't see or hear them, but they're always around."

"Not in this concentration, however," Askar interjects. "Since we've become visible, we've found it difficult to live in peace out in the wider world. Here we can go about our days unmolested, gather our thoughts, reflect."

Mama scoffs.

"So, the Testing made you visible all of the sudden?" I ask.

Askar shakes his head. "It was gradual, over the course of years. People have always felt our influence, and have normally been responsive, but when they began to see and hear us more concretely, things changed. They began to resist us. They no longer interpreted our desires as their own, and yet these desires felt so familiar to them, they couldn't bear to have us around."

My confusion must be clear on my face, because Askar continues: "Yes, we're devils, but once we became corporeal, we became more like you. We can be threatened. We can be hurt."

"So, you came here for safety?" My mind reels at the idea of devils in danger themselves.

"We are not so very different from you now. We all need somewhere to live. And once we find security and sustenance, we all have higher needs to serve. Hence this," he says, gesturing out toward the prayers. "We all want the same things: pleasure, community, sense of purpose, love—"

"Devils know love?" Mama asks, incredulous.

"Of self, certainly."

"But otherwise?"

Askar tilts his head. "Does anyone?"

"We are all the heroes of our own stories," murmurs E.

"Indeed."

The gremlin scurries up to our host and says something in its growly language. Askar nods then says to us, "Asphodel rightly reminds me that it's time to ask you to step inside, for your safety."

I look at Mama, whose continual state of suspicion is at an even sharper pitch. "What's going on?" she asks, eyes narrowed.

"Please do not be alarmed, you aren't in any specific danger. It's just that at certain hours this city becomes a bit unpredictable. We don't recommend being outside, even up here, but you will be quite safe downstairs."

An army of gremlins begins to cart away the buffet and break down the tables. One of them snatches my plate from my hands.

"Hey, just a—"

Askar's face darkens and his voice lowers, sending a feeling of worms crawling through my guts: "You are being reseated downstairs. Now."

Mama hands her plate to a gremlin and we head for the stairs. The gargoyles, however, aren't coming. E is leaning over the railing looking down at the courtyard. M is off in a corner in quiet conversation with something that looks like a squat, scaly weasel.

"Aren't you coming?" I ask.

M raises his head but doesn't even bother to look in my direction. "We'll be along," he says dismissively.

"Aren't they in danger too?" I ask Askar.

"It's difficult to say. We haven't hosted gargoyles before. We'll keep an eye on them."

Just like when I was younger and Mama sent me to bed while she stayed up, I'm annoyed that E and M get to stay up on the rooftop.

"This will just be for an hour or so," Askar informs us. "If you like, we can notify you when it's safe to come up again."

Mama gives me a look that tells me we'll be long gone by then, weapons or no. "No, that's all right," she tells him. "We'll be fine in our room."

Just before she takes the stairs, she turns to face Askar once more. "You say devils always lived among us humans. Angels too?"

"Certainly," he answers.

"So where are the angels?"

Our host looks out over the courtyard. "Your kind asked too much of them. They didn't survive."

FROM: Joseph Evans
TO: Manfred Himmelblau
CC: Meena Gupta

Subject: In the City of Cringing Blankets

Transcript of interview with Tad and Margaret Swanson (TS and MS), proprietors of the Do Come Inn near Silver Springs, Nevada

Location Notes: It's a small, parched town, full of modest split-level homes, many abandoned. As far as commerce goes, not much more than the Swansons' motel, a diner, a gas station/convenience store, and an ammo shop flanking the dusty highway that runs through town. In one of his emails before our visit, Tad wrote that people used to come through here on the way to the Lahontan Reservoir before it dried up, canoes strapped to the roofs of their cars, kids and fishing gear in the back seat. *After the Springs went,* he wrote, *so did the Silver. But thanks to the blankets, Marg and I get by.*

TS: They didn't ask to be woven, these blankets, and if they had, they wouldn't have asked to be brought to this city. These blankets are watching, and they have seen some things. To be sure, there have been some happy things, some titillating moments as well. These blankets have also seen some horrors.

MS: It's not that our visitors don't realize they're being watched. People actually plan their arrivals carefully; hardly anyone stumbles into town unawares. The strict prohibition against videotaping is what maintains interest in our city. One can take all the pictures one likes, but a picture of a blanket scrunched up into itself isn't the most thrilling of photos.

Such photos could've been taken at home, no need to have traveled so far to the City of Cringing Blankets.

TS: There's nothing special about how our blankets look or feel or smell: standard cotton poly blend, an unremarkable off white that blends in with any décor, pleasantly fluffy, smelling faintly of dryer sheets or unscented upon request. They are, in fact, so unremarkable that a salesman once tried to sell us these sew-on tags that would designate each blanket as one of the cringing variety. But we said *No thank you, sir, the proof is in the cringing.*

MS: Some of our guests unpack first, making a note to experiment with the blankets after they've had a bite to eat or explored the city (there is a bit of shopping and dining down the road). Others, however, will make a few half-hearted attempts before they head out for a drink, say by cricking their hands into claws and roaring in a misguided attempt to *frighten* their blankets. Others might pull down their pants to moon the bedding, or feign a slap in the blankets' direction. Blankets have been farted on, kicked, pulled off the bed and stomped on, but none of these techniques work.

TS: We don't have surveillance, mind you. People tell us what they've already tried when they ask us how to trigger their blankets.

MS: What these blankets really react to, as all visitors come to understand, is shame. Not their own—how could a blanket feel shame? No, they react to the shame of the guests.

TS: If you felt a little embarrassed about mooning your blanket, then you would be able to observe it shrink a bit into itself, its edges wrinkling slightly toward the center. But really, how many people feel shame lowering their pants in the privacy of their own rooms? A little sheepish, perhaps, at the idea of trying to humiliate an inanimate object, but that isn't the same thing as shame. So they will try again, each attempt leading to a more extreme measure, each flicker of a blanket's hem inspiring an even more outrageous ploy to get a stronger reaction.

MS: Just as it can be tempting to raise one's voice to be understood in a foreign country, there is a common inclination to shock a blanket into cringing. Blankets aren't prudes, however, so mere lovemaking doesn't trigger them. Couples trying new things, on the other hand, to the extent that they feel a flicker of shame, begin to see a reaction. Individuals traveling alone devise their own methods, sexual or otherwise, some involving copious amounts of food or alcohol, or new special friends. To be clear, at our establishment all luggage is screened for small animals. We are not *that* sort of place.

TS: Given the currency of shame for blanket-cringing, we advise families not to visit, as that rarely ends well.

MS: Breakfast at our inn tends to be a quiet affair. Lovers are either exceedingly polite toward one another, to the brink of formality, or quietly fuming. Friends stare in opposite directions, looking anywhere but at each other.

TS: When our guests check out, we can tell whether they've achieved their goal in the City of Cringing Blankets—if we see them at all. Larger establishments would offer express checkout, allowing guests to leave on their own time without having to face another human soul. But as a Mom and Pop shop, we still pride ourselves on our personal approach. We want to know whether our guests had a pleasant—or at least, productive—stay, whether their visit had been all that they'd hoped, if they'd seen everything they'd hoped to see. The guests who look up for more than a second may redden and quirk their lips in a brief, polite smile. Others may blink back an unfortunate thought. Some can only stare, reflecting the shock they discovered inside their rooms—and themselves.

MS: Then they depart and, eventually, write their reviews. Anonymously. As unpleasant as it can be, we read them to make sure we're offering the best possible service. We aim to please, and helping people learn a little something about themselves is satisfying, in its own way.

TS: Still, every so often while turning over rooms, we find a blanket that won't unfold. Even after a wash and dry, despite our shaking and pulling, it remains puckered between our hands, unable to release itself from what happened in that room. Then it's almost like a shadow travels through the fibers of that blanket into our skin. Once that happens, every blanket in our presence cringes and coils until they're all twisted hopelessly in upon themselves, and we have to call in help to put everything right.

MS: Still... This is our livelihood. We have obligations, after all: to our staff, to our community, to our children. To uphold our way of life. This is what we repeat to ourselves, our voices soft and low, until the blankets around us settle and let us untangle them, allow us to smooth our hands once more over freshly-made beds, leaving not one wrinkle behind for our future guests to see.

FROM: Meena Gupta
TO: Manfred Himmelblau
CC: Joseph Evans

Subject: In the City of Gurgling Windchimes

Transcription of notes found scribbled on a stack of bar napkins and backs of envelopes, in Stillwater, Nevada. Artifacts coming to you via post.

Location Notes: The name "Stillwater" is a cruel irony in this town: there is hardly any water left. The breezes that stir the windchimes also rattle the dried grasses around the bed of what used to be the Stillwater Point Reservoir nearby.

It's going to happen any day now, we can feel it. We've been working and saving and paying and paying and paying, and after all that working and saving and paying, how could today not be the day? Or tomorrow. Soon. At some point, our windchimes will chime again: the one with that sweet high crystalline tinkle, the other with its mellow knocking of hardened bamboo, the third, that relaxing clacking of shells. We'll hear those sounds again, soon. We just have to be patient. And keep paying.

Which means more working, and we're happy to work. That's what we've been doing this whole time, and we're prepared to keep on writing the emails and going to the meetings and editing the reports and achieving (when possible, exceeding) the metrics, and doing the evaluations and memorizing the statistics and forgiving each other for a late birthday present here, a forgotten anniversary there, because we've all got our eyes on the same prize: we just want to hear those windchimes chime again.

The gurgle we hear now isn't so bad, once you get used to it. And boy, have we had the chance to get used to it, ever since that first milestone when we got our degrees. The ceremony was magical, all of us in our caps and gowns, the tinkling of our accomplishments on the breeze. As each name was called, each of us walked across the stage to collect our diploma and our chimes: silver for undergrad, gold for doctorates, platinum for law school. After the ceremony we posed with our chimes, slung them over our shoulders as we sipped champagne at the reception. When we got home, we all hung our chimes up on our parents' porches, beaming as each puff of wind sent the music of our achievements through the neighborhood.

We knew the chiming wouldn't last forever, and yet we were surprised at how quickly the tinkling changed, sinking, slowing, morphing from crisp airy chiming into a low, guttural gurgle, with just a hint of a scratchy, genderless voice. The primary feature of the sound was its own obstruction, some unseen impediment of a moan we strained to recognize. There were no words, only a gargle emanating from the chimes.

We ground our teeth in our sleep, dreaming of that choking tone. Our parents worried and hung flower baskets around the windchimes, perhaps hoping to block some of the breeze, but there was never any question as to whether they'd keep the windchimes on display. We'd earned them, after all.

Fortunately most of us got jobs. Of some sort. Eventually. We received our second set of chimes as we walked into our workplaces. Some of us with the platinum windchimes got a new set of chunky, mahogany chimes so long we had to hold them above our heads to keep them from dragging on the ground, so large we had to move out of our parents' houses to hang them, so heavy we had to hire someone to help attach them to the porch roof railing. Even now, on windy days, we worry about how long they will hold.

But that was the minority of us. Most of us got those medium-sized bamboo chimes with a pleasant, mellow tone, perfectly fine for that point in our lives, not what we'd have given someone for a wedding or anything like that, but nice enough to put out on our parents' porches next to our silver or gold ones. If a couple of us went in together, we could rent our own place, so even if we didn't have a porch, maybe there was a little ledge we could attach them to, or we could at least bring them with us and still know they're there in a box in a place we had a right—as long as our lease held, anyway—to call our own.

Which was fine, really, because we were too busy working and paying to give much attention to the chimes. We already knew what would happen: the nice, satisfying clunk of bamboo would become less pleasant over time, turn harsh and brittle, halting, clogged, until it guttered into the same gurgling our first chimes had adopted. We didn't even have to hang them to know, because we'd heard it happen to friends or older siblings, and anyway, our parents prepared us for the turning of the chimes by telling us not to be disappointed when it happened, that it happened to everyone, heck it happened to them, but after the job chimes they got the marriage and family chimes, which were also sweet for a spell, which, yes, is hard to imagine now that they're gargling too, but not because of us, no, we shouldn't blame ourselves, and anyway there's nothing to blame anyone for, because that's just how it is. It's nobody's fault, especially not ours.

So, once our own chimes turned, we didn't have a problem packing them away, though we must admit, we did take them out from time to time, say, when we earned a promotion or won an award, or made a breakthrough on a really important project, to see if a little of that original, clean, clear tone would come through, and if we heard it, we'd find a place to hang them for a little while, even if just in our rooms, prodding them with a finger to hear them tinkle and click as we drifted off to sleep. And if that brief spell got us through the next few days, weeks, months of working and saving and paying, then we'd take it.

And for some of us this was enough—but who were we kidding, not really, because once the tinkling and clinking turned back into gurgling, and we stuffed our chimes back into their boxes, who among us didn't consider trying for their next set of windchimes? We knew they wouldn't look the same for everyone—in fact, we were banking on that. God knows even those of us who wanted the marriage and family chimes knew we wanted them to look different from the strings of cracked shells hanging from our parents' porches, gurgling in their own hacking way.

So when we stepped up to the altar/nursery/either/both in whichever order it happened, and accepted our own strings of shells, we comforted ourselves by noting the ways in which they differed from our parents': ours were cowrie, not puka; ours were natural, not dyed; ours were tied, not drilled; ours were hand-gathered by an indigenous vegan feminist art collective, not churned out in some sweat shop in Bangladesh. The only thing we didn't compare was how long it took for the first crack to develop, or when the pleasant tradewind click of shell against shell began to drawl and rasp into the gargle we knew so well.

Some of us keep them up for appearances. Some of us hide them away in frayed cardboard boxes up in the attic, still grinding our teeth at their churn in our dreams—not that we remember the dreams, but the ache in our jaws betray them throughout our days of working and saving and paying.

Still, we know there's a point to it all, and we know it's going to happen any day now. Things will change: we'll pay everything off, and then magically our shoulders will sink from around our ears, and we'll know it's time to pull down the rickety ladder to the attic, or descend the creaking stairs to the basement, blow the grime off the boxes, and listen to our windchimes sing once more.

It's coming. We've heard the cheerful tinkle of a thousand shining windchimes wafting down from the largest houses on the hill, homes owned outright, their porches jingling with the accumulated chimes of generations. And it amazes us how much sound so few homes can make, how their chiming can carry so far across the city, because every once in a while, when the breeze hits just right, even those of us in the darkest of basement apartments can cock an ear and hear it. *And if it happened for those up high on the hill,* we reassure ourselves in those moments, *surely with enough hard work and saving and paying, it will someday happen for us too.*

Won't it?

FROM: Meena Gupta
TO: Manfred Himmelblau
CC: Joseph Evans

Subject: Proposed detour

I think it's safe to say at this point that the trip has taken a bit of a demoralizing turn. It's almost like this was supposed to be psy-ops—but I refuse to believe they'd be testing that kind of thing here. I can't let myself believe that.

If it's all right with you, we'd like to skip the City of Sobbing Candles and go straight to the Swordfighting Robots. Joseph's pretty excited to check that one out.

IX.

I can't believe they just… left.

I circle the room in which Dolores and Rose were supposed to have slept, looking in the empty closet and under untouched beds.

M stands at the door, sighing. "Are you finally ready? We've wasted enough time already."

I'm well aware of that—I was the one who said we should let them get their rest. Turns out they weren't even here.

He snorts, impatient. "You didn't think we were all going to stay together, did you?"

"No, of course not. I…" I feel stupid because I was looking forward to telling Dolores we'd finally found it: the city of gargoyles. Well, we haven't found it, but we know it exists. There are more of our kind out there.

"But they don't even have their weapons." I point to the knife and spear lying on the bed. "They'll be vulnerable."

"They'll get more. Humans always find a path to violence. Come."

I follow M down the hallway and to the stairs—which he unexpectedly begins to climb.

"Don't we need to go down?" I ask.

M laughs and tells me to trust him. I follow him up to the rooftop.

"Climb on," he says.

I look down over the courtyard, with its unending bustle and muttering of praying devils. Above us, hot blue sky. "I'm saturated. You can't carry me."

"Our hosts have given me a parting gift, an elixir that will give me enough energy to get both of us off to a good start."

I narrow my eyes.

"You don't trust the gift of a devil, yet you worry about the two women who abandoned you? You've been around humans too long." He huffs air through his nostrils with a grunt. "E, don't you remember what it was like, when it was just us back at the church?"

And I do. I remember how it was to be among our own kind. Even when there wasn't enough water, even after hours of near-fruitless foraging, we'd still feel better when we returned and settled along the walls and leaned on one another. Vlad, Beatrix, Winsome, Quasi, Horatio, Maximilian. We belonged together.

"We always had your stories to look forward to," I say.

"But it wasn't just that; we kept each other alive, exchanging moisture until we all had the same amount. We didn't even think about it."

"At first. But things changed."

"Only once we had nothing left to give." M unfolds his wings. "But when there's enough water, things will be better. The way they once were."

It all sounds too perfect. "How do you know?" I ask. "How do the devils know there will be enough water?"

"They told me we will want for nothing, and I believe them. Do you believe in me?"

I hesitate. "Do you even know what direction to fly?"

"Generally. Get on."

"Fine," I say, wrapping myself around M to distribute my weight. "But I still think we should stop if we see Dolores and Rose. I'll bet they'll help us—we helped them, right?"

"Oof, someone's gotten heavy," M says with a smirk.

"Wait, we should bring their weapons."

"Stay put. I can only carry so much weight, and someone's been hitting the water pretty hard latel—"

"All right, Cat, shut up or I'll swallow you whole."

M laughs and flaps his wings with a vigor I haven't seen in weeks. My heart soars as he lifts into the air.

FROM: Joseph Evans
TO: Manfred Himmelblau
CC: Meena Gupta

Subject: In the City of Swordfighting Robots

Transcript of interview with the Husk Family at the Husk Family Compound, precise location undisclosed by request.

Location Notes: We can't say much, but as you know, money means water, so if you see satellite imagery of an astoundingly lush oasis in the middle of a desert in the general vicinity of Middlegate, Nevada…

Also, this really was transcribed from an interview. These people actually spoke this way, almost like they were programmed… Fascinating.

JE: I'd like to thank you for meeting with us—

EDWARD HUSK: The sounds of battle echo through the streets at all hours: the clank of metal on metal, the scrape of steel on stone, the thudding of robots marching on until they find one another, assume the stance, *engarde*, then one or the other makes the first advance, calculating probabilities, categorizing risks, having already mapped out stimulus and response so many times that every thrust or parry is one of a series of predictable outcomes. The only variables now are tripping on a crack in the sidewalk, or crashing into another pair of dueling robots. Humans have long since been killed or fled the city, never able to out-calculate their robotic foes.

JE: I see. And how did—

ELAINE HUSK: The ones who first translated the ancient craft of sword-fighting into code were not warriors themselves. Despite the lifetimes of video games that inspired them, they were no match for the robots, and any remaining joy of creation melted away with the contents of their bowels when they had to hoist a real sword against the enemies they had made. The creators, being crafted neither of pixels nor metals, didn't last long.

ELIJAH HUSK: We must clarify, this isn't one of those stories where the robots gain sentience and decide to take over the world, no matter how much better they might be as its stewards. These robots aren't even all androids—they don't all look human. They are machines with recursive code that tells them to fight, to defend their encoded selves no matter what forms they take, say a toaster or a blender or a refrigerator or television or car, each unit as dimly aware of itself as any organism that knows it must defend itself against aggressors. And if there are no aggressors around, it must find one.

JE: Okay, but—

ERIK HUSK: Unlike other animals, however, these encoded beings have only the knowledge of swordfighting. They will pass up other weapons, stomping or rolling right by guns and hammers and crossbows (it was always a strange city) and picking up anything that can serve as a sword. And after all of the cosplay swords were broken in battle, and the few true swords as well, they began using new implements such as swiffers and plant stakes, shovels and spades, and when all of those were finally broken as well, they began tearing the crossbeams out of buildings and ripping lead pipes out of the ground (it was also an old city).

JE: Interesting. And—

ELIZABETH HUSK: At first, most citizens were merely a bit unsettled, believing that only those who kept swords lying around the house were in any real danger. When the people asked us, their leaders, if the robots should be stopped somehow, we assured them we were studying it—as, the irony does not fail to dismay by now, we'd previously studied the dangers of crossbows and lead pipes. Those who could afford to leave the city center at that point did, hiring their own swordfighting robots for protection and providing them so many swords they would never have reason to enter the shiny new bunkers they had been newly programmed to protect.

JE: And those who couldn't afford to move?

ETHAN HUSK: Some tried to plead with the robots to stop fighting, but that wasn't in their programming. Those people didn't last long.

Others tried to reprogram the robots to only go after the wild animals that had begun to enter the city to feast on carrion, but again, that simply wasn't in the robots' programming. Those people didn't last long either. Neither did the animals.

Still others stayed for the show, climbing high for the best seats, and they all thought it was pretty entertaining until the rooftops they stood on came tumbling down for lack of crossbeams.

EUNICE HUSK: Quite a number of citizens tried to justify the robots' actions, explaining that this was simply how they were programmed, reasoning that there must be some kind of logic determining who would be killed and who wouldn't, and if they could only figure it out, then perhaps they could avoid being killed.

ERNEST HUSK: But they were killed too.

EVELYN HUSK: And after all of the humans and animals were killed, the only other moving things left were the robots themselves. And because they were programmed to fight, they fought, and still do so to this day.

JE: Why has no one stopped them?

EASTON HUSK: Well, because they have been granted the right to swordfight. The only course of action, then, is to observe them from our shining bunkers. As long as the streets echo with the clash of battle, we will record every fallen robot; and as long as they continue to cull their own, we'll have time to plan for whatever comes next.

ELEANOR HUSK: When only one robot is left standing (or rolling, or hopping), we assume it will continue its directive to swordfight any moving thing, and since it will be the only moving thing, perhaps it will begin to fight itself. We are keenly interested to observe which move will prevail: thrust or parry, kill or be killed.

ELLIOTT HUSK: All of the lives, human and machine, that have been and will continue to be lost are regrettable, but our hands are tied. There is much we don't know: will these robots operate beyond their current base? Does their programming contain the directive to go out to a new city once they raze the last? We have no way of knowing. Those who wrote the code are long dead.

ELLA HUSK: All we can say with certainty is that the robots were created with the inalienable right to swordfight.

ELLIS HUSK: And as such, it is for us merely to observe and hope—

EMILIA HUSK: by god—

EVAN HUSK: to survive.

FROM: Meena Gupta
TO: Manfred Himmelblau
CC: Joseph Evans

Subject: In the City of Leaping Libraries

Transcript of interview with Ida X. Wellington (IXW), Librarian in Schurz, Nevada

Location Notes: Despite what the interviewee says at the beginning, Schurz seems to be a relatively peaceful place. The havoc initially wrought by leaping buildings has been smoothed over, rubble cleared away, plants sprouting up through cracked asphalt. Perhaps the admonition is a way to keep too many visitors from staying and straining the resources? I, for one, could see myself settling down here after retirement...

IXW: I wouldn't recommend moving here, though I've grown used to it by now—I suppose that's because I'm one of the librarians. I move with the library when it leaps. I'll never get crushed when somebody wonders a wonder, or wants to read a book they don't already own, or when someone's computer breaks down and they need to apply for a job. Whichever library's closest to them will uproot itself and fly through the air, landing next to wherever the person is.

MG: That sounds a little dangerous.

IXW: It is. I mean, the libraries try to avoid landing on other things. But I'll admit it: in the beginning, people and pets were crushed, buildings demolished. Knowledge is power, all right, and sometimes it can be destructive. And whoever wondered or asked or thought or needed, it was a struggle to convince them that it was still okay to borrow that book or fill out that online application after finding out what their curiosity had led to.

By now, the libraries have worked out their landing spots. I know when I land, I'll either be in the northernmost corner of the city park, or the parking lot behind the train station, or on the riverbank on the south side of town.

MG: But how does that work? I mean, how do you manage not knowing where you'll wind up each day?

IXW: My husband and I used to own a condo in Northwest, but it became easier to just live here in the library. Sometimes we look out the window at the end of the day to see where we are and decide where we want to eat. Since we figured out that the libraries never leap after closing hours, we've never had to worry about coming back from dinner or a movie and finding our library gone.

MG: Wow. So would you say things have stabilized by now?

IXW: Mostly, yes. Things are quieter now. More people are using e-readers and search engines, but not everyone has access to those things, and plenty of people still need help, or simply a safe and quiet place to sit and think. And now we've reached an agreement with everyone left in town. No more random wondering, no more willy-nilly wishing. When they find themselves pondering things they don't know, they say to themselves *Next time I'm at the library I'll look it up.* Then they'll gather their lists, their scraps of paper with ideas scribbled on them, their notebooks full of questions and ideas, and they'll stand near the closest crater, safely outside the ruin of cracked blacktop or torn-up grass, and just before they hear that telltale whoosh of wind, that shudder of glass in its panes, that rumble and creak of concrete and steel, they'll close their eyes and think: *I wonder.*

FROM: Meena Gupta
TO: Manfred Himmelblau

Subject: Between you and me...

Okay, so, knives, guns, fighting robots, even the floating wolves, it's all starting to track—but weaponized libraries? I don't care who we're not supposed to be talking about here; if I'm right about this, how do we help fix it?

FROM: Joseph Evans
TO: Manfred Himmelblau
CC: Meena Gupta

Subject: In the City of Shrieking Ottomans

As in Carson City, certain acoustic realities precluded the effective recording of interviews. Thus, I offer a creative response based on our experiences.

Location Notes: Hawthorne, Nevada is actually a lovely large town/ small city with a modest but vibrant urban center surrounded by calmer suburban areas for families. Like Schurz, Hawthorne is refreshingly stable in terms of resources and quality of life—if one doesn't mind a little noise.

Every travel guide one reads beforehand warns that it will be difficult to relax in the City of Shrieking Ottomans. Every time one sits down at the end of a long day of walking or shopping or sightseeing or whatever one does while visiting cities, in *this* city one can't simply put one's feet up and sink into a moment of calm. In the City of Shrieking Ottomans, the least bit of pressure upon almost any footrest engenders a piercing, horrific scream.

It doesn't matter what kind of footrest it is. From a true ottoman—a full-blown, round, upholstered, overstuffed extravagance—down to a humble wooden footstool, any use of an inanimate object to rest one's foot or feet upon will be rewarded with a bloodcurdling shriek. The scream doesn't immediately disappear as soon as the weight is removed, either. That would be too forgiving. No, the offending footrest-er must endure not only the dreadful yowling, but also the scowls of everyone in the vicinity for the several minutes it takes for the shrieking to subside.

After two or three shrieks, the average person begins to hesitate before even sitting down. But the sitting isn't the problem; the propping up of feet on any article of furniture is.

Research reveals that residents of the City of Shrieking Ottomans simply do not own any. Neither ottomans nor footrests nor even coffee tables can be found in the homes of the city's denizens. Over time, inhabitants have found various alternatives to ottomans that don't engender shrieks: stacks of books, piles of laundry, empty boxes, even sturdy pets can serve the purpose. The trick is, they can't be permanent. Books must be swapped out, laundry must be washed and folded, boxes replaced with more recently acquired receptacles, and even the most foot-friendly dogs need a rest (there is a much-sought-after breed of Setter that seems born to this task, sturdy and contact-hungry, and pups have been known to go for tens of thousands of dollars).

The tourist areas, as one might expect, are completely different. There one finds all manner of ottomans: round, oval, square, and rectangular; velvet, leather, silken, and natty; brocaded, tufted, quilted, and studded; striped, spotted, and solid; ottomans with and without storage, with and without legs, lowered and raised—each with a different tenor of shrieking. One ottoman emits a single, high-pitched peep of a shriek upon encountering the weight of resting feet; another cries out in a deeper, more masculine tone. The largest ottomans feature entire choruses of agony.

For children there are brightly-colored, polka-dotted models that emit shrieks of delight ending in giggles. *See,* one says to oneself, as though trying to convince—whom?—*it's not all bad.*

Admittedly, however, most of the shrieking is horrendous. The locals who work in the touristy parts of town wear headphones with anything from calming music to heavy metal—one hears a wide variety of music blasting from their headphones when they remove them to help visitors. One knows to wave them down for assistance, due to their printed smocks reading "Please raise your hand for service" in a dozen languages. Eucalyptus aromatherapy wafts into the air from misters placed at regular intervals throughout the old town, an effort to counter one sense with another.

The problem is, a waiter mentions (beginning with "no offense, but…"), as the town has become more popular, businessowners have acquired more shrieking ottomans. Additional bars, restaurants, and attractions have sprung up, all featuring more opportunities for visitors to rest their feet. There is one silver lining, however, the waiter says: homeowners have gradually moved farther away from tourist areas, opening up opportunities for young families looking for affordable starter homes.

Most visitors can only bear to spend one night in the City of Shrieking Ottomans before moving on in their travels. There are some, however, who stay, mainly because they're on a budget—for certain auditory reasons, this city turns out to be a reasonably-priced sojourn for those who are willing to stock up on earplugs and persevere, spending most of their time away on day trips. (At least, that was the plan my traveling partner and I had agreed upon.)

Some visitors, however, prefer to remain right in the thick of it, embedding themselves in the symphony of screams for days on end, whiling the days away in cafés, resting their feet on shrieking velvet ottomans, sipping their mochas while resting one leg atop the other, then switching again, tilting their heads as the pitch changes with every shift of weight.

This certain type of visitor will linger, taking his evening meal with his feet resting on a wailing footstool under the table, keeping always at least one foot pressed against moaning wood from appetizer through dessert. After dinner, this sort of visitor will retire to a cigar bar or jazz club, where he'll barely be able to hear the music over the howling of the embroidered ottoman propping up his feet as he cradles a tumbler of scotch, sipping occasionally, but mostly resting the rim of the glass against his bottom lip as his feet rest on a shrieking stool, the screaming, it seems, an accompaniment to the wail of a horn over thudding drums, the heel of his foot almost an extension of the band, pressing into the crescendo on stage, holding a certain tone a half-step lower, wringing the most out of the grating screech under his heel to prolong a dissonant chord. He will play this human voice like an instrument. This visitor, impresario of agony with sparkling eyes.

The lovely innkeeper once said—she used to share more in the early days, before she reluctantly extended this visitor's reservation, before his traveling companion took the car and moved on without him—that in the many years she'd run her establishment, there were still some visitors who shocked her anew. Sometimes she thought about moving away from the kind of city that would draw such people to it, but then, she said, she realized that there were such people everywhere in the world. At least here you could tell which ones they were, she said, and she'd advised this visitor—back when he first arrived—to be wary of them. She said you could see which ones to steer clear of by watching their eyes: scanning, hungry, eager, searching for the next thing that might scream in agony under their feet.

It was the kind of thing, she sighed, you could only sense when you saw them in person.

At least now she knows which kind she's dealing with.

FROM: Meena Gupta
TO: Manfred Himmelblau
CC: Joseph Evans

Subject: In the City of Kissing Dragons

Transcript of Interview with Rose Baker (RB) and Dolores Baker (DB), mother and daughter traveling through Lee Vining, California

Location of City being described: Black Marble Village (unincorporated), Klamath National Forest

Location Notes: There's not much to say about Lee Vining—it's little more than a supply hub, a place for travelers to take a break and stock up on food, water, and weapons. This interview was unplanned: I was just in the canteen refilling line when I struck up a conversation with the Bakers. They said they'd been traveling all night, trying to escape what they said were gargoyles who had taken them hostage—of course I had to get that story. I wasn't quick enough, though, and by the time I got their permission to record and we found a place to sit down, the mother had moved on to another story about an incident from her teenage years in the City of Kissing Dragons.

RB: Was it passion or fear that cost us our home? Was it hubris? Or was it sheer laziness? I've never told the full story of that final day, not even to my daughter, but now [gesturing at microphone] it's time. Maybe one day you'll figure out where the dragons came from in the first pl—

[RECORDING INTERRUPTED]

RB: All right, then.

Cinders rained down on that final day. Embers spewed from steaming nostrils. Forked tongues slid against one another. Some dragons kissed in flight, looping upward from the mountaintops, curling around their partners; others kissed while writhing on the ground, generating earthquakes with each rough tumble. They kissed in twos and threes and occasionally by the dozens, slithering and rubbing in orgiastic clouds of smoke.

DB: Dang, Mama, kissing dragons? Why didn't you ever tell me any of this?

RB: Well, simmer down and let me.

MG: Pardon me, when you say "kissed"…

RB: I mean kissed. Like men and women do [looks at daughter] when they're older. And no, dragons are not natural kissers. These beasts were enchanted, bewitched by dark human arts. The people of our village found it too troublesome to keep killing dragons one by one, year after year— and for what, the dragons would have argued, for merely being hungry and feeding on livestock and children who don't listen to their mothers?

[looks at daughter again]

So our council met and debated, finally agreeing upon a spell that would draw the beasts toward a different kind of hunger, one that would distract them with passion for one another to the exclusion of anything else: eating, drinking, anything actually required for their survival. They would kiss until they wasted away and died. Everybody said it would be the nicest way for them go.

DB: Spells? You're casting spells now?

RB: Not me. Pipe down and listen, girl.

The council ordered one last individual slaying, required for the spell. The dead dragon's heart was carried up the winding mountain path to our temple. Spiceweed was burned and the adult townsfolk called out to our goddess of fertility, asking her to inflict a heightened version of human desire upon our dragons. They chanted and danced. They covered each other in rose oil and kissed. They [pauses and looks at daughter, then clears throat] did things only consenting adults do in a haze of incense, and their heat rose up on scented, oily clouds to find the nostrils of every dragon in the land.

Drawn by our goddess, the dragons gathered over the mountains surrounding the altar, making it their new mecca of mating. At first we thought they were attacking one another, but we soon understood it for what it was: kissing. Dragons were not meant to kiss, but our plumes of smoke had been filled with human lust, so the dragons began adopting human ways. Their tongues sought each other out, forcing the dragons to open their mouths to one another, these mouths meant to pluck livestock from hillsides, to bellow at humans with spears, to erase us in torrents of flame. These mouths meant to reap, to consume and destroy, were suddenly called upon to give pleasure, maybe even to love.

Of course, they didn't—give pleasure, or love. The dragons were still dragons, and could only comprehend kissing as taking, as possession, or consumption. They wrestled, mouths splayed, teeth ripping, blood streaming, saliva dripping and singeing rock below. Their bodies coiled as they grappled, scales glistening and shedding onto the mountaintops like snow.

And still more dragons gathered, summoned by the spell, until there was no more room for them over the temple. From our village, we watched them spread out through the air, kissing, twisting, belching embers, growling, shedding, spilling their caustic blood, flying closer and closer until they soared right above us—above those who had dreamt up the spell.

Sparks rained down upon our village, setting rooftops alight. We fled burning buildings only to meet the sting of dragon spittle.

We looked up into the rain of dragon blood, pressing our ears against the huff and bellow of dragons mid-kiss. We wiped the sting from our eyes, gathered our belongings and fled the flames of the only homes we'd ever known. Long after the fire reduced our village to ash, dragon scales tumbled down, a flurry of glittering fat flakes.

We decamped to tents just outside the city, hoping to go back and rebuild once the dragons had spent themselves. But mating occurred: the females only stopped kissing long enough to lay their eggs, many of which were destroyed, rolled on and crushed, or disintegrated under dragon drool, but enough survived to hatch and perpetuate the race. These dragons no longer needed to eat. They adapted to the human invention of kissing, subsisting on passion alone. They left all of us and our remaining straggle of livestock in peace, but there was no way to survive the destruction of their love.

[Long pause]

Now that place is barren—for humans. As far as I know, dragons are still wheeling in their terrifying knots overhead.

I still dream about them sometimes, wheeling above the wrecked shell of what used to be my home, twisting, bleeding, peeling, howling, clamoring, dripping, drooling—

[RB stands suddenly]

I have to—there are some more things we need.

DB: I'll come—

RB: No, stay here and mind our supplies.

[RB walks quickly away]

MG: Is she okay?

DB: Yeah. She just needs a minute, I think… I've never heard that whole story before. She doesn't like to talk about her past—you can see why. But I think I know what triggered it: a few weeks ago she thought she saw a dragon, which is scary, sure, but now I really get it. She was so rattled she dropped her canteen, which was like, yikes, I mean she would have laid into me if *I'd* dropped half our water supply, but the gargoyles eventually gave it back, so—

MG: Okay, wait, hold on. Your mother saw a dragon—now, not back in her village—and then gargoyles took your canteen?

DB: No, she just thought she saw a dragon. It was dark inside the barn, see—we were looking for supplies—and this thing rears up and unfurls its wings and we jet out of there. But it didn't come after us and I wondered "Was that really a dragon?" but she said, "Use your head, girl, the wings, the claws, the serpent-like body. Those teeth." But all that was really just E protecting M—

MG: Hang on: E? M?

DB: Those are the gargoyles. E is like a serpent with feet, M is basically a lion with wings. And I can see how they looked like a dragon, E standing in front of M.

It's like they dredged up all this old stuff Mama never wanted to talk about, like the [REDACTED] years ago. Nothing has been the same since, she says. She's seen some things.

MG: I understand... So, she's told you about some of these places?

DB: Bits and pieces, stuff like floating wolves and sailing statues. Those were after the thing with the dragons, but before the place where the crazy bats chased everyone out of town. She'd had me by then, but I was so little I barely remember it. Just the flames.

MG: Wow, I really need to talk to your mother.

DB: Yeah, you and me both. [pause] But I can tell you a little about Oakland; I mostly grew up there—until it flooded. After that we spent some time in Los Angeles and Joshua Tree. It was pretty there—until it burned. We've been traveling ever since.

MG: Incredible. I'd like to hear more, especially about the gargoyles— but you said you're heading out again?

DB: Yeah, to Carson City.

MG: Shoot, I'm going the other way. Big Pine.

DB: Don't. Seriously, don't go there.

MG: I'm supposed to meet my colleague there. It was next on our list.

DB: For real, don't. It's too dangerous. We barely made it out. If the gargoyles hadn't been there—

RB: [returning with a spear] Dolores, take this. [Hands her a knife in a leather sheath] Get your things. We're going.

DB/MG: [general confusion/commotion] What? Why?

DB: Ms. Baker, I'd really like to—

RB: You've already got your story. We have to go now.

DB: You saw them, didn't you?

MG: Who?

DB: The gargoyles.

[simultaneously]

RB: Gather your things. Don't forget your canteen.
DB: But Mama—

MG: Maybe I could come with you, at least part of the way? I'd like to know more about—

RB: No, that was enough sharing already. Stay safe.

DB: But Mama, she said she's going to the place with the bonfires.

RB: If you know what's good for you, you won't. [walks away]

MG: I appreciate it, Ma'am. We'll figure something out. [whispered] Here, Dolores, take my card. I want to talk to you and your mother. You're the first people I've heard talk about gargoyles, so—

DB: Sure, I—

RB [calling from distance]: Dolores!

[END INTERVIEW]

FROM: Meena Gupta
TO: Manfred Himmelblau

Subject: Request

I'm sorry, I know we weren't supposed to split up, but I just couldn't take it anymore. Joseph kept steering us toward the weirdest cities on the roster. I'm trying to be a supportive colleague, but I didn't see the need to stay in that ottoman place after we'd completed our observations.

I'd planned to wait for him in Big Pine (again, another one of his picks in our itinerary). But… would it be possible for us to keep on researching separately? He says he's fine walking and bumming rides. I just don't know if we're the best traveling companions.

And by the way, I'm assuming the dragons and gargoyles were no accident—the lack of control over them was. We've got a lot to discuss.

X.

It's amazing how things can twist and turn: one day we were in the City of Praying Devils, soaking ourselves with water to our innermost pores, discovering that more of our kind have survived; the next moment we were flying, looking for clues. And now we're well on our way to the City of Dancing Gargoyles—well, at least to Carson City, which is as far as Rose has agreed to let us accompany them.

We must be close, because we're finally walking on something other than sand. It's a road, cracked and rutted, forcing me to thread a path around holes and random chunks of asphalt—but a road. A sign we're on the right track.

From there, we're on our own.

Dolores takes a generous swig from her canteen. "Things will be better in Carson City," she says. "It's bigger; there's more jobs there. Mama can get work as a cook, and I can waitress."

M says, "I'm sure we would find your mother's cooking delicious— if we ate food." He's been friendly toward the humans since we regrouped, and I still find it unsettling.

"And they'll have better maps," Dolores continues. "We'll find one that shows where your city is." She kicks a chunk of asphalt. "Then I suppose you'll be on your way."

"That was the deal," says Rose, glancing back for a moment without slowing down. She tolerates our presence, likely because other travelers keep their distance when we're around. And by now she's given up on trying to keep her conversation-starved daughter from speaking to us.

Dolores glares at her mother's back, then says to M, "I'll miss your stories, though."

"Well, we're not in Carson City yet," he purrs. "And there's a story I heard once from a cluster of rose petals blowing by on a gust of wind…"

Reenergized, M's been entertaining us with tales he's heard from swallows and flies, from honeybees and butterflies. Some of them I've heard before, some I haven't, and I wonder how many of them are true.

"This is one I wouldn't share with just anyone," he says, glancing at her mother up ahead, out of earshot. "But I think you can handle it:"

Once upon a time, and ever since, there were maidens who'd had enough. They'd simply had enough, these maidens, enough of the warnings, the exhortations to be mild, to be chaste, to behave, to be beholden to every wish a society could impose upon them. They wondered:

"What if we said what we wished for, what we really wished for, and what if it had nothing to do with a prince or serving our fathers or pleasing our mothers or being beautiful or helpful or mild, or even remotely polite? What if we said what we really thought about fairy godmothers and spinning wheels and mattresses and peas?

"What if we said… what if we said… what if we just said?"

And so they did, they just started saying and saying and saying. And the more they said, the more they came up with to say, like:

"What if I told you the wolf was actually a sensitive lover and an excellent provider to boot?"

and

"You have to have a firm hand with dragons, show them who the alpha animal is. What all those knights get wrong is…"

and

"The King is actually from Ohio. He was a used car salesman before he became Regent."

And it got to the point that no one could tell how much of what the maidens said was actually true, even if they claimed to know it for a fact.

But the maidens just kept on talking:

"The princess is suuuuper flexible. I heard it from a stablehand..."

and talking:

"She knew they would put a pea under there. She was faking."

and talking:

"It was shoddy workmanship. That idiot pig should have bundled those sticks into fasces. Worked for Stalin—not that I'm excusing the murders."

and they kept on talking:

"You do know that marriage is just a financial transaction, right? It's like, you for a few cows or a sack of gold. What a racket. The fools don't know we'd be worth more in the work force."

and talking:

"Protecting your maidenhead with bashfulness is great and all, but have you tried wielding a sword?"

and talking:

"Jack's a goddamn idiot. Doesn't matter which Jack."

and talking:

"There's video footage: Aurora was asleep. She could press charges."

and talking:

"You know what all those Crusaders got wrong? Everything. Every. Damn. Thing."

and they wouldn't stop:

"Belle just needs to admit she's more into the Beast than the Prince. No shame in that. Many people don't know this, but Beasts are some of the most generous and attentive lovers out there. You know who else is a fabulous lover? The Kraken. I shit you not. Here's what happened: I was kidnapped by pirates once and..."

They simply wouldn't stop talking:

"Give me a sextant and a sailboat, and I'll take you places you

couldn't imagine. Nothing to it. Most people don't know how to manually navigate the seas anymore, but it's the easiest thing in the world."

And to this day, they have not stopped talking.

In fact, not many people know this, but the City of Blustering Maidens isn't so very far from here. I could take you there. I mean, reading books is great and all, but have you ever tried swinging a sword at Don Juan, or telling a Crusader exactly where he can stick his cross, or discovering all of the ways a Kraken can love?

By the time M finishes, Dolores is smiling. She kicks another chunk of asphalt so far ahead it almost hits her mother's boots.

M laughs, and there's something in his eyes, some glee behind his throaty chuckle that's deeper than the tale he's just told. I know M. He's chosen quite a clever story to share with her—daring, grown-up, all about independence—she no doubt feels acknowledged in some way, perhaps sees the story as a mirror of herself. But what's in it for him?

Some secret machinations are going on beneath that shaggy stone mane of his. I'll just have to trust him to tell me in good time.

FROM: Manfred Himmelblau
TO: Meena Gupta

Subject: RE: Request

I'm sorry that balance has been an issue, but I must implore you to stay together. As you are finding out, the dangers of these cities are unpredictable. Please avoid Big Pine until I can gather more information about these bonfires.

Joseph has contacted me. He has managed to find his way to Bloody Mountain, but has no other transportation, and I must insist that you go meet him there (I'll forward his email to you in a moment), after which point you will choose the next location to investigate. I will ask Joseph to be more attentive to balance in terms of the emotional intensity of your work together—but keep in mind that there are only so many options for pleasant visits on your itinerary.

Thank you for alerting me.

And yes, we will have a full debrief when you return.

Manfred

FROM: Manfred Himmelblau
TO: Meena Gupta

FWD: In the City of Bleeding Books

------------Forwarded Message--------------
FROM: Joseph Evans
TO: Manfred Himmelblau

Subject: In the City of Bleeding Books

Location Notes: Bloody Mountain, California. It's true, what they say. It's all true.

These are books that don't want to be held. And yet you do, and here you are, wishing, perhaps, that you had never come. Your hands are sticky and red, and you've barely cracked the first cover. This book might once have held a confession, a cry for mercy, a plea for help. These books are sopping and fragmented, and it is your task to put them back together.

You have come to pick up these books, to scoop slimy red pages up off the floor, to reconstruct them and figure out which memory goes where, which war to which era, which genocide to which land. You will read the pages, and as you read they will straighten, unwrinkle themselves, knit themselves back into order and become plain. One by one, the books will remember themselves and stiffen, spines will reveal themselves, and as each title reappears you will find a place for it, clear a spot in the gore on the shelves with a sweep of your palm, and slot the book in, still bleeding, but now whole.

All around you are sodden red piles, books that need sorting, pages slid out from dissolving covers. The air smells of copper and pulp, the floors are slick, the shelves endless. You peer down the aisles receding endlessly into the gloom and try to recall how you got here.

Others working farther back in the stacks have long since forgotten why they came. There is so much to be done, so much to repair, so many things that need to be read and saved, you know there will never be enough of you to do it all. You don't even know if you're reassembling the most important things.

Look at this other traveler, reading and sobbing, smoothing pages, shuffling them around until they settle into place. There's no one to tell him if he's done it the right way. He spent decades preparing, studying and conferring, only to find that so much is not as he thought it would be. By now he can't be sure of anything, and yet he continues to work, scooping up page after page, reading, smoothing, solidifying what he can. We can only hope his motives are pure, his methods correct.

Is he crying because the task isn't what he'd expected—or because it's exactly what he'd feared? Or perhaps he weeps because there is so much yet to save, so many more bleeding books to put back together, no matter how much it hurts. Every person is needed for the work that will never end.

And you: how did you get here? Why are you here? Is it some sort of penance; are you seeking justice; did hubris call you to this task? Or have you merely lost your way?

Even as the last question forms in your mind, you realize none of them matter. After everything you've seen, the "why" is immaterial. Bloody pages, bloody hands, this whole wretched, bloody world. It's all come down to you to sort it out.

FROM: Meena Gupta
TO: Manfred Himmelblau

Subject: RE: FWD: In the City of Bleeding Books

Thanks for forwarding this to me. You're right; I'll go get him. I've rejiggered our itinerary, and I know just the place to take him next.

MG

XI.

M and I lounge in the fountain in front of "our" church in Carson City. It feels impossible that we have access to this supply of water whenever we want it, and a new home in the belltower as long as we care to stay. The only downside is the pastor staring out the window at us. He's thrilled to have actual gargoyles at his church, but sometimes his gawking is a little too much for me.

"Want to head to the café?" I ask.

M preens in the water. "I'll pass, thanks. Give the ladies my best."

With an awkward wave to the pastor, I climb out of the fountain to visit Dolores and her mother. I go via side streets, giving a wide berth to Market Square and its crying merchants. We almost left because of them, but if you stay far enough away from the square, the wailing becomes background noise, like the wind when we were up on the church wall.

When I walk into the café, the happy tinkle of the bell above the door and the smell of Rose's bread are the first things that greet me. It almost makes me wish gargoyles could eat. It's almost empty now, between mealtimes, and only a few people sit scattered at a couple of tables, staring warily at me as I enter. Then Dolores sees me, stops wiping down a table and calls me over.

"Have a seat," she says. "I was just about to go on break."

She pulls a chair out for me, then sits down across the table, stretching out her legs. I climb up and try to copy her pose. Furniture still baffles me.

"Pastor creeping you out again?"

I chuckle. "M loves it. Finally, a chance to be appreciated after all of those centuries too high up on the wall to be properly admired."

"Well, both of you *are* pretty unusual. I mean, you're the first living gargoyles I've ever met. Speaking of which, any leads?"

I shake my head.

"Me either," she says. "But I'll keep asking—no matter what M says."

For some reason he's become pricklier about talking to anyone else about the city of gargoyles. But how are we supposed to find it if we can't ask?

"So… I have a question." She hesitates. "I hope you don't mind my asking. So, M's mostly lion, right? So when I talk about him—well, I call him 'him.' Because he has a mane—but is that right? Is he a 'he'?"

"Yes, he goes by 'he'."

"And what about you?"

"Well, I wasn't carved either way, neither 'he' nor 'she.' Gargoyles like us go by 'it'." I pause, trying to remember what I've heard humans call me. "Rose calls us 'it'."

"Yeah. But when she says that…" Dolores scrunches her lips to one side. "I mean, humans use the word 'it' for things. Objects. But you and M aren't just things, you're people—or I guess 'beings'—with your own minds, your own personalities. I mean, I'll call you whatever you want, but when people say 'it'… Well, I just thought you should know what that means."

"Oh, I see." It smarts a little, how people still view us. But it's not a surprise. "Well, what do you recommend?"

"Well, how about 'they'? There are lots of options, but I hear 'they' the most."

"'They.' Sure, I'll try 'they'."

I'm glad Dolores told me about *it* vs. *they*, but I also feel a bit foolish finding out about this just now. M, eavesdropping on humans for decades with his keen hearing, probably knew the difference the whole time.

I sense Dolores perk up as she looks toward the entrance. A few young men wearing Lake Security uniforms amble in and head toward a table. I'm relieved it's not that other group of men, the ones who come in and hunker around a table grumbling about everything that has changed in the world—like, say, gargoyles. For a while, according to Dolores' manager, they used to carry huge rifles strapped against their backs, until Security asked them not to. Now things have "stabilized," meaning they've downsized to handguns in holsters.

But today it's just Lake Security.

One of them looks over at Dolores, smiling, and she blushes. Just as she's about to get up, her mother comes out of the kitchen, wiping her hands on her apron and calling out, "What can I get for you gentlemen?"

Dolores heaves a sigh and sits back in her chair. "She always does this. She's so overprotective."

I look over at the young men, but she hisses at me not to look. I turn back to her quickly. "Are they dangerous too?"

A sly smile sneaks across her face, then disappears. "They're not supposed to be—they're Security—but I suppose they could be," she says, contemplative. "Any man could be. But that's why you have to actually talk to them, get to know them. Figure out if it's the kind of danger you're looking for." The smile reappears.

For a moment I'm utterly confused, but then it clicks. "Ah, Rose is afraid you'll have a baby."

Dolores laughs. "Oh my god, E, you're just like Mama: instantaneous conception. The way she watches over me, it'd have to be airborne. Or telepathic." She leans forward, crossing her arms on the table. "So... do gargoyles ever...?"

"What, mate?" Now I have to laugh. "No, that's not how we're made. It looks uncomfortable, actually."

Her eyes widen. "Wait, you lived on a church. You've seen people...?"

"I'm talking about animals. Yes, all over the place. People, we've only heard."

"In a church?!"

"You'd be surprised. All that yelling. How can that feel good?"

Dolores slumps forward theatrically. "Well, at this rate, I'll never know." She looks over at her mother taking the young men's drink orders. "I love her, but... I need to live my own life, you know? We've been together day and night for so many years—keeping me safe, she says—"

"Well, we have seen some pretty strange things out there."

"Yeah," she sighs. "But it's not just dangerous cities and things. She's always trying to keep me away from other *people*. Men, in particular. Starting with my dad." She digs a fingernail along a crack in the wooden table. "I guess he was pretty... abusive. I don't remember because I was too young, but it was bad enough that she had to leave, and I'm glad she did, but now..."

I stay quiet, just listen.

"And yes, there are bad people out there. But not *everyone*. You and M turned out to be okay—I mean, after stealing our water."

She smirks at me, then glances over at the table of young men. I look over too, just in time to see the one with curly black hair smile at her again. She looks down at our table, even redder than the first time.

"Anyway, it's pointless. Every time we have to move, whatever community we had just scatters and we have to start all over making new friends. Sometimes it seems like Mama doesn't even bother trying anymore. If we had money, we could just move somewhere safe and stay there. But folks like us..."

She goes quiet for a moment. "Whatever. It is what it is, right? At least I can help you and M find your home."

"Thank you," I say. But sitting here with Dolores, saturated with water, surrounded by smells of bread and beer, I find I'm in no great rush to leave.

FROM: Meena Gupta
TO: Manfred Himmelblau

Subject: Reunited

I got him. He's okay—I think. I'll steer us toward some restorative places. We could both use it.

FROM: Meena Gupta
TO: Manfred Himmelblau
CC: Joseph Evans

Subject: In the City of Flying Trumpets

Transcript of interview with Daniel Rodriguez, resident of New Paradise, California

Location Notes: I wish I could stay here.

DR: Sometimes they arrive in the morning, gleaming in new sunlight, heralding the wonders of the day to come, soaring in formation across the sky like a flock of golden geese on their migration. But, unlike the birds, this sparkling brass never forsakes us—or, it never did until...

Well, the trumpets haven't entirely forsaken us. We still see and hear them arcing overhead with their glorious tidings, which you've come to hear. How long are you here?

MG: We're uh... we haven't really decided yet.

DR: Well, if your dates are flexible, you're sure to hear one of their fanfares. Most likely. There will be eleven trumpets in flight at a time, though I'm told there are many more of them overall, each one with its own slight variation in color, shape, and tone. Myself, I can't tell. For all I know, they just change positions within the V, but musicians say they can hear the difference between the different ensembles, and who am I to second-guess the experts?

I wish I could tell you exactly when they'll appear. They used to come with the sunrise every morning, shouting their flourish into the skies, a salute like something you'd hear at an Olympic opening ceremony: proud, majestic, stirring. Lots of what they call "tongued triple notes"— we've all learned a little music-speak after so many years of airborne concerts. I suppose even the trumpets knew it was a splendid thing to be alive another day.

Aside from some disgruntled night owls who moaned about losing sleep, we all greeted the horns with a smile. The trumpets used to come once in the morning, and at least two or three more times during the day, because someone was always getting married, or having a baby, or getting a promotion, or falling in love, or leaving a toxic relationship, or getting their driver's license, or remembering to call their mother when they said they would.

MG: Wow, they seem to come out for lots of things.

DR: Yes, I suppose it sounds like a lot. But as large as the city is, no one heard every single pass the trumpets made. It was simply encouraging to know that somewhere above the city, a formation of trumpets was celebrating someone's good fortune. I mean, you have to figure at least someone's got a birthday every day, right?

MG: Sure. But excuse me: you said earlier that they "used to come' multiple times a day. They don't anymore?

DR: Sadly, no. Some say it was drones that changed things. It was bound to happen at some point, I suppose. Birds weren't an issue for the trumpets, possibly because they both traveled in Vs, but the more things people started using drones for—picking up coffee, delivering groceries, making sure their kids weren't smoking out in the woods—

the more the flying things got all tangled up. Accidents happened. Drones and horns started falling out of the sky onto rooftops and gardens, parking lots and, occasionally, through windshields. Rich folks found drones sputtering around in their illegal pools (we knew they still had them behind those tall walls).

Fortunately no one was getting injured, so it was either annoying or amusing—depending on whether it was *your* windshield or the one on the show-off's vintage Jaguar next door, if you know what I mean.

MG and DR: [chuckling]

DR: Things took a turn when the mayor's teacup poodle met its demise in the bell of a fallen flugelhorn. City Council had to do something in earnest then. Thing was, no one really knew where the trumpets had come from; there was no one in particular to contact. Private drone users were on the defensive, of course, adamant that their rights not be curtailed; not to mention the lobbyists for all the mega corps promising instant deliveries. Some think they planted a seed somewhere, started a stealth campaign about noise from the trumpets. Bit by bit, people began hinting that the trumpets always *had* been a bit annoying, and were technically not in compliance with the city noise ordinance, particularly those heralding the sunrise (given the hour). And if the corporations had to abide by local ordinance, people began asking, shouldn't the trumpets too?

Well, you know how it goes: the question of who kicked off the grumble campaign didn't matter once it caught on. And although we still didn't know who was responsible for the trumpets, the city decided that action was necessary. Citations for various noise and airspace rules were issued and folded into airplanes, then launched by a clerk out the window of the top floor of the municipal building. The citations were, according to the subsequent City Council report, carried off on an improbable gust of wind so high the clerk lost sight of them (he'd intended to follow the path of the citations and pick them up where they landed so as not to litter, for which he would have had to cite himself). For a while, it seemed like nothing had come of it, but then we began to notice that something had indeed changed.

First, the sunrise salutes stopped occurring on weekends, and to be honest, a lot of us were glad for the chance to sleep in. Over the following weeks, the trumpets reduced their sunrise appearances even further, to only Mondays, Wednesdays, and Fridays. After a few months, they just happened once a week, and now it's not even that often. Now the trumpets only announce the most objectively beautiful sunrises, and when that happens we all get up and look out our windows for a glimpse of something truly special. It's been a bit cloudy this week, though, so I can't say for sure if that will happen while you're here. But if it does, do yourselves a favor: get up for a look. It's guaranteed to be worth your effort.

MG: You mentioned birthdays as a trigger. Mine's coming up soon. Would the trumpets come if I celebrated early?

DR: Well, Happy Birthday in advance! But sorry to say, that doesn't seem to be a sure thing anymore either. You might try looking up wedding announcements, because the trumpets normally still appear for those ceremonies—in fact, it's considered a bit of a bad sign if they don't.

MG: So, what are the guaranteed occasions when the trumpets come out? I mean, a new baby, surely?

DR: Oh yes, everyone gets to be special at least that first time in their lives, but births are a little difficult to predict. I suppose you could hang out in front of a hospital and wait for a pregnant woman to arrive, but is that really how you want to spend your vacation?

MG: It's not really a—never mind.

DR: Well, regardless, it's hard to tell now when the flying trumpets will come out. And yes, it is a bit sad. But I think the uncertainty also makes the moment that much more special. Now, when we hear the trumpets' salute, all of our moods lift at someone else's good fortune. Someone is tasting their first moments of life, or having their first kiss, or graduating from school, or getting their first paycheck, or their doctor is telling them they're cured—someone somewhere is experiencing a wonder. And we never know exactly when we'll hear that fanfare or see those gleaming horns in the distance, and while some folks don't miss the constant "noise," others are a bit sad not to share in it more often.

The way I see it, though, it's more like inspiration. If you want to hear the trumpets, want to look up at their brassy flash and sparkle overhead, and you know they will come out for special moments, then ask yourself: what can you do to coax them out? What would make this a special day for you? If you want to see the trumpets, go out and find them. Anyone can do it—it's just hard to know how sometimes. But I hope you do. And when I see those trumpets fly across the sky, what a thrill it will be for me—for all of us—to know that somebody out there has found their bliss.

FROM: Manfred Himmelblau
TO: Meena Gupta

FWD: In the City of Feasting Banshees

Meena? Can you explain? He's not returning my emails.

------------Forwarded Message--------------

FROM: Joseph Evans
TO: Manfred Himmelblau

Subject: In the City of Feasting Banshees

We sisters want no more of this mad meat,
these feasts of famine sliding down our throats.
We red-eyed, sorrow-bloated banshee folk
crave nothing more than silent, deathless peace.

We've had our fill of misery and war,
our bellies churning, bursting with your grief,
we keen in supplication for relief
from glutting on mortality and gore.

We wail, you say, and Death comes close behind,
as though you did not know Her or Her power,
as though we, and not She, could choose the hour
of your undoing. Your bind is our bind:

She walks at night; we shriek our fruitless warning,
then chew the glistening gristle of the mourning.

FROM: Meena Gupta
TO: Manfred Himmelblau

Subject: RE: FWD: In the City of Feasting Banshees

Thanks again, Manfred. No, we didn't go anywhere like this. When I asked him about it, he said he was just filing another report from something he read in the City of Bleeding Books.

I'll keep an eye on him.

XII.

"Wow, that was really hurtful," says E. "Did you hear what it called me?"

The gargoyles and I are standing at a railing overlooking a rarity: a lush valley full of palm-like trees and huge ferns, populated by the world's most vulgar dinosaurs. Obviously my boss didn't know what he was talking about when he told us about this city full of creatures "just like E and M."

"You know," I say, "none of them actually know what they're saying. And I'll bet it's a 'she'."

"Still... 'scrawny little bitch'?"

"How can you tell it's a she?" asks M.

"I'm just guessing by the feathers." I point first at the foul-mouthed dino with brownish feathers, then to another similar animal with tinges of blue in its plumage. "See, hers are less colorful than the other one's there."

Just then the brighter dino opens its mouth: "The fuck you lookin' at?"

I laugh, which really gets them going, stalking back and forth shouting, "Fuck right off, assholes!" and "Sons a bitches, go to hell!"

E shudders. M's got thicker skin—but then, he *is* made of stone. I wish people would just try to get to know them. Even Mama's okay with them now—in her way.

"Lemme at those motherfuckers," a dino screams.

"We'll rip your fuckin' hearts out!" yells another.

I flip open the brochure. The people at the Visitor Center said all their dinosaurs were herbivorous. Sure enough, there it is, right under *Safety*. I read it out loud to E: "*All of our dinosaurs are bred for maximum visitor safety. Only herbivores were selected, and chosen from species that will grow to no more than 250 pounds.*"

E stares at the two dinosaurs stalking and swearing down in the valley. "They're awfully hostile for vegetarians."

"I remember you getting pretty salty when you tried cutting bugs out of your diet."

E side-eyes me.

I consult a sign on the fence. "It says 'Pantydraco,' but I don't think that's what these guys are."

"No, these dracos are definitely not wearing any panties," says M.

A fresh volley of insults roars across the chasm:

"This motherfucker."

"Sonofawhore!"

"Imma rip your goddamn panties off and choke you with 'em."

The gargoyles and I look at one another, eyes wide. Dinosaurs of all sorts thunder up to the railing: brontosauruses, triceratopses, velociraptors, things I don't know the names for—and a tyrannosaurus rex.

"How did they—" M asks.

"But I thought—" I say.

"Bite us, bitches!" comes the answer from The Valley of Swearing Dinosaurs.

I swallow, hard, as dinosaurs thunder toward the walls at the edge of the valley—toward us. "They can't…can they?"

"No," says M. "The walls are too tall."

"Or they would be if…" E points out how the sauropods are forming a sturdy base, with beefy theropods piling on next. "Now all the ornithopods need to do is scramble up and—"

Suddenly, an ear-splitting alarm erupts and chaos ensues. The gargoyles and I rush for the exits as emergency vehicles race past us toward the valley. Behind us, we hear a bunch of snarled expletives, human and dinosaur alike.

This is so not good.

So why am I giggling? Why are M and E and I grinning at each other, why are we all now laughing so hard we can barely catch enough air to run. I look behind me—so far they've managed to keep the dinos from breaching the valley wall, but I'm not about to stick around and find out.

"Whatever you do," I yell, "don't tell Mama!"

The gargoyles and I keep running and laughing, out past the Valley walls.

It's dusk by the time the bus drops us off in Carson City. I don't feel like going home yet, so I suggest we all go to the café. E doesn't say anything, but I'm sure they suspect who I'm hoping to see there: the guy with curly black hair. Ben. I overheard the other Lake Security guys say his name. We've been eyeing each other for weeks now, both of us too chicken to make the first move. Not to mention, Mama's watchful eye has been kind of a buzzkill.

We step up to the entrance just in time to see Ben on his way out with his colleagues, and I know it sounds corny, but when I see him, everything else fades into the distance. He says something to the other guys, and they go on ahead without him. Meanwhile E pulls M inside, saying something about getting us a table. Ben and I are left at the door, staring at one another. My heart beats faster, and I don't know what to do with my hands, so I stuff them into my pockets.

"Dolores, right?"

I've suddenly forgotten how to speak.

"Sorry, didn't mean to freak you out," he says. "I'm not a stalker."

His voice is deep, and his dimples even deeper. I manage to talk before I melt. "I promise I'm not a stalker either—Ben."

He chuckles. "I see we both have our ways of finding things out. Things we want to know more about." He stares at me, his smile sly, his gaze traveling from my eyes to my lips before locking on my eyes again.

"Seems so." I lean against the wall, hoping to hide my giddiness. I know I should say something more, but I don't know what.

"You going in for a shift?" he asks.

"No, just… here with friends."

"The gargoyles," he says, nodding. "See, this is why I want to know more about you: what kind of badass is friends with *gargoyles?*"

I laugh. "We met on the road. Everyone's scared of them, but they're actually really nice." Mama's voice in my head stops me, chiding me for being so transparent. Nobody else needs to see through our protection. "Well, they're mostly nice," I say, recovering. "As long as you stay on their good side."

"I'll try to stay on their good side, then." Ben leans against the wall next to me. "You met on the road—from where?"

"Oh, a few places," I say, keeping it vague.

"A few places. I get it; I've been there. But you're sticking around here for a while, I hope." He turns toward me, one arm against the wall. His eyes are light brown with flecks of gold.

The door opens and Mama pokes her head out. "Dolores, E and M are waiting for you."

"I'll be right in." I stifle a groan. "Sorry, I should go."

"E and M," he says. "On first name terms with gargoyles. Impressive."

I pry myself off the wall and reach for the door. "What can I say, I'm a woman of mystery."

"Wait." He takes a step toward me. "So… I'll see you around?"

Do I dare? My head feels light but I say it anyway: "I get off at 8:00 tomorrow."

His smile widens, and I fall a little bit in love with the one front tooth slightly overlapping the other. "I'll see you at 8:00, then."

I'm already counting down the hours as I float into the café.

FROM: Joseph Evans
TO: Manfred Himmelblau
CC: Meena Gupta

Subject: In the City of Lying Houses

Transcription of audio from visit to Dyer, Nevada (Somehow the name of our host eludes us. I'm certain we asked at some point, but neither of us can recall it.)

Location Notes from DYER, Nevada: I mean, just say it out loud. That's all you need to know.

Host: Some of the houses claim the most horrific abuses: children tortured, women grievously harmed, animals set on fire. None of it's true, of course, in the City of Lying Houses. None of the muffled weeping from within this bubblegum pink bungalow actually happened. Screams like those emanating from the attic of the Victorian next door were never screamed, and the body parts flung out on the lawn of the leaf-green split-level house across the street are just a mirage. Look closely, they're merely red tulips.

The mansion on the hill, however… Do you see it, that bright gleam up there on the hill? Let's go, it's not actually that far away. These houses lie, remember? They make themselves look bigger, make distances appear greater than they are, make the hill seem steeper than it actually is. That one on the right, for example, the cream-colored ranch style home with blood seeping from between its vinyl slats? Lies. The family who lives there just had their third baby, and all of the children are very much alive.

Through the window, you can see them sitting down to lunch.

And that one up ahead, the cabin with natural wood stain: ignore the black smoke curdling out of the chimney, spreading the most noxious odor. Also a lie. See, the owner is coming out his front door right now to play fetch with his dog on the lawn. In addition, those "ashes" you're brushing off your shirt—merely pollen. You must simply look closely enough to see the truth. These homes cannot sustain their falsehoods forever.

Come, we're supposed to be heading up the hill anyway. It's best to keep your eyes straight ahead, focus on your goal, so as not to get sidetracked by untruths.

And with that, we've already arrived at the edge of the property. See how the mansion's marble glitters in the sun? The walkway was purposely designed to wind, so you can view the home from all sides: elegant columns, generous windows, French doors opening onto the rolling back lawn. Such a striking contrast between the white columns and the lush, green grass, don't you think?

[Splashing water, soft strains of a harp.]

Note the dual dolphin fountains spouting on either side of the walkway to the front door. Modeled upon fountains at Versailles, I'm told.

The harp is coming from inside. Come, let's listen. Yes, right through the front door—it's already open, you see.

I love watching visitors take in the mansion for the first time. It can be overwhelming, so I suggest beginning with the sheen of the polished floor, appreciating the slate-colored seams running through the milky white marble. Let your eyes move up to the mahogany table with its lush centerpiece of white freesia and roses—do you smell the hint of eucalyptus underneath the floral notes? Now look beyond the flowers and let your gaze sweep up the elegant, broad stairwell to the balustrade on the next level. From there it's natural to look all the way up to the vaulted ceiling (that's why the harp echoes so beautifully) and observe the light glistening off the cut-crystal chandelier.

Whatever's baking now smells delicious, cinnamon and vanilla, a hint of allspice. And do you hear that?

[Children's laughter, faint.]

It's coming from upstairs—let's take a look. It's all right, no one minds.

Note how the stairs are perfectly placed for a comfortable ascent. One can just imagine the lady of the house gliding up and down like a queen.

[children's giggling continues]

It sounds like it's coming from everywhere, doesn't it? The nursery is this way. It is a charming room, so warm and comforting, full of teddies and binkies and blankies, with a mobile of plush suns and moons rotating over an empty crib. But no one is here.

That's the playroom across the hall, also empty, as are the bedrooms next to it. All of the bedrooms are empty. But laughing children aren't sleeping, so that's to be expected, isn't it?

[Sounds of a party floating up from downstairs, music switches from harp to jazz, adult conversations burbling over saxophone.]

Ah, there's nothing like jazz to lend an elegant touch to a gathering. The family had excellent taste in music, in art, in everything. And they did love their soirées.

Oh my, do you smell that? Whatever was baking is beginning to burn—you see, the house is already beginning to give up its ruse. But there's no one in the kitchen to check on it. No, there's no point in going downstairs. As I told you before, nothing is—

Very well, if you insist.

Watch your step going down, the lighting has dimmed.

[Muffled voices: harsh, arguing.]

I wish I could tell you what they're saying, but I can't understand them either.

[Yelling. Crying. The music cuts out.]

What a shame, the floral arrangement in the entryway has wilted. Moldering flowers have a singular stench, don't they? It makes one almost grateful for the acrid smoke coming from the kitchen.

[A scream, sharp and brief. Breaking glass.]

That would be the French doors. Wait. Listen.

[The *clack* of a man's shoes on marble.]

No need to step aside, there's nothing really there anymore.

[Footsteps on stairs, fading.]

They're heading upstairs…

[Shrieking. A baby's cry, a thud, more knocking.]

[Silence]

There's no need to go look; there's no one left. I've told you, houses can only lie for so long.

Why are you shaking? Isn't this what you came to see?

Why does everyone who visits this city leave weeping?

FROM: Meena Gupta
TO: Manfred Himmelblau
CC: Joseph Evans

Subject: In the City of Philandering Flowerpots

Text of a sign at the base of a giant hibiscus bush next to a cute yellow house, representative of signs near various vegetation (plants, flowers, gardens) in Tonopah, Nevada

Location Notes: I wish I could stay here, too.

How, exactly, does a flowerpot make love? And how does a flowerpot betray? Technically, a pot is a vessel, able to receive more than one seed at a time. But there is more to philandering than that. There is also an act of seduction, a promise made that this union is special, that this flower and this pot—this *particular* flower and pot—*must* be. Perhaps the problem is that the flower misinterprets the pot's enthusiasm about *Now*, reading into it a promise of *Always*. This is the mark of a philandering pot: the awareness of this disconnect, the capitalization on the haplessness of a flower, for there is little doubt that the flower is smitten, committed root-deep to the flowerpot's earthy embrace. *And isn't the flower happy?* the pot will insist. *Look, it's bright, open, cheerful, completely supported and thriving in the sun. Isn't this just what the flower wanted?* The pot can't actually see the flower—it doesn't have eyes—but it can feel vibrations emanating from the plant's roots as they push, explore, plumb the outer limits of the world around them. Where roots meet the inside of the pot, they rest against its cool, dark cheek, curling into the curve. Is the pot to blame that it can't be infiltrated, that the tiny, reaching mycelia at every root-tip will never penetrate the glazed surface they encounter? It's not the pot's fault it's so well-protected, nor is it the flower's fault that it wants to dig itself into every pore of the pot's being. But is it really more of *the pot* it needs—or simply *more*? This flower wasn't meant to live in such limited circumstances, after all. It was meant for so much more than confinement. It must either move on from these fertile beginnings or stay and wither. And who can change this flower's fate? Who can flip the script and dig it free? You. You reading this sign, you are the gardener of souls in the City of Philandering Flowerpots. You are the one who will work your fingers into the soil, levering gently around the edges of the plant's known world, sliding daylight between root and pot, slowly rocking and rotating this universe, wincing at each little rip—when things have gone this far, roots coiled this deep, there will always be some hurt. But you feel the heft of the roots against the pads of your fingers, feel their compactness, their solidity. They're ready. There's nothing left for them in this pot, with its tenuous grip on the flower, so you lift it and carry it toward the hole you've dug into the rich, dark earth. There's so much more ground to cover out here in the wider world, and this flower has everything it needs to survive. You tip the clump of roots into your palm, press it into its new home. In sunlight, the flower drinks greedily from your watering can. The philandering flowerpot gapes, empty.

XIII.

Ben and I are sitting by the lake—it's small and manmade, but there's actual grass, a huge flex these days—with an impromptu picnic of bread and cheese, and a bottle of merlot. Sounds civilized, but no: we didn't plan for this, so we're slugging wine straight from the bottle and tearing hunks of bread off the baguette. At least I've got my knife for the cheese.

Is this "dating"? Are we dating? This is the second time we've arranged to see each other.

Is it dating if your mother can't know?

Like a telepath, he says, "Your mother's pretty protective of you, isn't she?"

"You noticed?" I say, sarcasm dripping.

"Can't blame her. Things can get pretty rough out here. I'll bet you've had some scrapes."

I think about the night in the City of Sneaking Fences, other times where we've had to prop a chair under a door handle to feel safe. Nights when we didn't sleep at all.

"Do you have a gun?" he asks, cutting off slices of nutty, buttery cheese and handing one to me.

This is like asking if I have wings. "No. She's against them."

He looks puzzled, so I explain: "She's not against them, per se, but they're expensive, right? It's not just the gun, but the ammunition, license, permit—"

He scoffs. "Nobody cares unless you start shooting."

"You've seen me and my mother, right?" I pull at my skin. "They'd care."

He nods. He's lighter than I am, but he knows.

Then I point to my knife. "You don't need a license for one of those."

"But you have to get close to use it." His eyes light up. "Or are you one of those scary knife-throwing warrior-queens? Battle-hardened, ready to kick some ass." Now he's flexing his muscles and pretending to throw knives, and he looks so ridiculous I have to laugh.

"I like your laugh," he says.

Which, turns out, is the quickest way to scare it off. I tear off a couple more hunks of bread for us.

"Not all guns are expensive," he says between bites. "And permits aren't required here. Wouldn't take much to get yourself a handgun, something easy to carry."

I scoff. "Have you seen how much they set you back lately? I mean, the legal ones. Mama doesn't want us to get mixed up with the kind of people who can get the cheaper ones."

He goes quiet. Birds twitter, and I can just make out the distant crying of the merchants in market square. Ben picks up the bottle and examines the label. "What 'kind of people' would that be?" he asks.

"I don't know. Gangs. Militia. Those guys who come into the café packing, talking big. People who don't care who gets hurt as long as they make a buck."

"Everyone's just trying to get by out here," he says quietly. He takes a swig and holds the wine out to me. "It's good that she's so protective. I just don't think she's looking at it the right way."

I snatch the bottle from him, annoyed. "She's gotten us this far." Even when we had to wedge a chair underneath the doorknob, we at least had a door between us and the rest of the world. Usually.

He holds up his hands. "Sorry, you're right. I didn't mean any disrespect. I just…" He trails a finger along the back of my hand. "I just like you, and I want you to be safe."

Ben takes my hand in his, and I thank god my palms aren't sweaty, because my face feels like it's burning up. His smile is so gentle when he strokes my cheek. I put down the bottle and we both lean in for our first kiss.

I haven't kissed a lot of men, but I've kissed enough to know he's good at this.

Really. Really. Good.

Like, lie-back-in-the-grass good, I-don't-want-it-to-end good.

Until I feel something wet on the back of my leg.

"Shit!" I sit up and my head spins with the wine and the kissing. The bottle is lying on its side, and when I twist, I can see the big red stain spreading down the back of my jeans. "Oh, crap."

"Oops."

"Yeah," I say, standing up. These are new pants, and Mama will start asking questions if I can't get this stain out. "I've got to take care of this." I eye the lake, contemplating.

"Uh-uh, I wouldn't recommend that, not in that water."

While he puts the rest of the bread and cheese into a bag, I pick up my knife and wipe it off on my jeans (may as well) before sliding it back into the sheath. "Go ahead and keep all the food."

"Getting rid of the evidence?" He stands up and holds both my hands in his. "You know, you're a grown woman, you're allowed to have friends. Boyfriends, even."

"Boyfriends?" The butterflies have completely taken over my stomach.

He leans down to kiss me again.

The wine stain can wait.

FROM: Joseph Evans
TO: Manfred Himmelblau
CC: Meena Gupta

Subject: In the City of Screaming Ropes

Transcription of audio from visit to Braeburn, Nevada

Location Notes: Didn't a famous author once say something about the past never being dead? Or even past?

It's not fair, really, the name our town has been given. It's not even a *city*, and we used to have a completely different name, something that ended in -ville; but no one remembers it, and every time we read it in the old records, we forget it again. So our name remains the City of Screaming Ropes.

The unfair part of it is the Screaming—very few of our ropes actually do. And they don't scream because they're in pain. How can an inanimate object feel pain? They scream because they're channeling the outrage of whatever they've been asked to contain. Plus, we don't even use those particular ropes anymore, the screamers.

No, most of our ropes only grumble while holding open a gate, or moan when we tie our horses to a hitching post. And we're compassionate people—we passed an ordinance against tire swings once we came to terms with the rights of trees. Sure, some of the purists *tsked* at the new playgrounds we built to replace the tire swings—which, they argued, were also made of wood. Wasn't it better, they asked, to hear a rope grunt from the burden of a living tree than to send kids scrambling all over the sanded-down bones of a dead one?

Well, we don't all agree on everything in the City of Screaming Ropes. But we do agree on the screaming: we don't want to hear it. Once a rope has been used to lead a goat, it's useless. Have you heard a goat scream? The whole reason you're using a rope is to get the animal to go somewhere it doesn't want to go. Its outrage lingers. It's uncanny.

Most of us will do pretty much anything to avoid touching ropes. Or if we must, we'll only use them for benign purposes. There was a time, before they began screaming, when ropes were used for all manner of things, day and night, benign and—not. In fact, there were some of us who loved the utility of a thing that could be used to swing one boy over a swimming hole by day, and another boy from a stout, dark tree in the dead of night. So practical, many would think. So versatile.

When the ropes first began making their utterances, we never knew which sound to expect when we touched one. We wondered why certain ropes would not choose to giggle at the thrill of flight and the joy of release into cool waters on a hot day, why they would instead decide to scream and moan, gurgle and gag. Whenever we discovered one of these unpleasant ropes, we tried to override its sonic burden with a more auspicious memory, using it to raise our flag up the flagpole every morning, or to hoist a new sign into place on Main Street, or to build a ladder up to a treehouse in the generous shade of an old oak.

Despite our efforts, there were certain recalcitrant ropes that insisted on screaming when we touched them. One by one, we picked those ropes up with shovels or pitchforks, and tossed them into the darkest corner of old Harley's tumbledown barn, left them there to gather dust and rot, never to be touched again.

Those ropes, however, refused to cooperate—over time they began murmuring again, all on their own. Harley said he'd hear mumbling and grumbling from the barn at all hours, even had the sheriff come out to investigate, but there was nothing there but those old ropes. We all told him to just ignore them, and for a while that was enough.

But the longer we left those unruly ropes be, rotting in the dank corners of the barn, the louder they got. Pretty soon you could hear them if you simply came near Harley's property, much less got anywhere close to the barn. Fortunately for him, he was going deaf by then.

But what about the rest of us? We can hear the ropes' wailing and carrying on clear into town these days. What are we to do? We can't go back and change the past. Plenty of folks want to go out there and burn the whole barn down, ropes and all, but Harley won't stand for any fires on his property. His boobytraps and his loaded shotgun have settled the matter.

And so we continue playing with our children, raising our animals, hoisting our flags, and running our businesses using only our most pleasant, dependable ropes. We go on humming and whistling, trying not to hear those old, untouched, unexamined ropes howling and moaning in the musty gloom of Harley's barn.

If we keep on laughing, we barely hear them scream.

FROM: Meena Gupta
TO: Manfred Himmelblau
CC: Joseph Evans

Subject: In the City of Chuckling Roses

Transcription of writing on found sheets of lined paper, perhaps journal entries, found in Crystal Springs, Nevada. Photos attached, originals coming via post

Location Notes: This would be a fine place to live as well.

Savannah finds them "charming," if a bit weird, but that's why she wants to go. We watched the videos together and heard all the chuckling. Each variety was different. She said the magenta ones reminded her of how her brother half-laughs when he doesn't want to admit her jokes are actually funny. The purple-pink roses chuckled like her teacher watching the mini-vids her class made as part of their history finals. *We still had to write papers*, she said, *but Mrs. J is coming around.*

She said the yellow ones sounded like her mom when she's with her dad—she loves that her parents are still so into each other. *Like, they're married, but they're also best friends*, she said, and I nodded as though that were something I'd ever seen before.

When the video showed the deep-red roses with scalloped petals, Savannah said they giggled like her mom when her dad's being all *gushy*; but when she said it she was smiling and scrunching up her nose, because deep down she thinks it's cute. She calls her parents *cute* when they're together, but what she doesn't say, doesn't need to say, is that she likes it because it makes her feel safe, because she knows they'll stay together, because this is what love can be.

I want to be happy for her, admire her confidence. I want to go with her to the City of Chuckling Roses, but if we do, I'm afraid I won't really hear anything she says because when we watched the videos, the magenta roses sounded like my dad every time he laughed at me and told me to learn how to punch, and the yellow ones sounded like my mother's sad laugh all those nights my sister would ask if he'd left for good this time; and the deep-red ones cackled like him when he'd come back home stewed, fouling the air with sweat and menace; and the mixed ones laughed like I did every time Mom said *That's it, we're leaving*, because we never, ever did.

So I'm afraid I won't hear anything my girlfriend says in the City of Chuckling Roses. I'll just be concentrating on calming my breathing, on keeping my hands still, on not ripping every last flower off its stalk and trampling them in their beds.

I have until tomorrow morning to decide: do I disappoint her now by begging off the trip, or disappoint her later by failing to contain my rage? Or even later, like failure-to-propose later, or marriage-and-kids later, or drinking-my-feelings later, or cheating-and-lying later, or you-made-me-do-it later, or only-staying-for-the-children later? And which of those laters would count as giving-things-a-chance later, and which would be keeping-her-tethered-to-a-broken-man later? I've seen all these laters before. What's to stop them from happening all over again?

Tomorrow morning should I just get up, shower, and follow Savannah to the train?

Should I bust us up by staying home, or bust us up by going?

She's always loved flowers. Seems fitting to let the roses decide.

XIV.

When M and I arrive in Schurz, there's already a small group of people, maybe a dozen, gathered near a line of cracked concrete. Two children walk in bored circles around their mother, who holds a tote bag lumpy with books in the crook of her arm. An elderly man pages through a well-used notebook, muttering questions about Gothic architecture to himself. Two young women about Dolores' age hold hands while they wait.

She should be here too. Dolores was the one who recommended this city, so I'd assumed she'd come with us. But it seems she's too busy with her new boyfriend—of course, we're not supposed to mention that to Rose, because Dolores told her she would be with us today. Apparently this is what people do for one another when they're friends. I'm not thrilled about this aspect of human friendship.

It looks like we've gotten here just in time. No one's really in charge; there seems to be an unspoken agreement amongst those gathered. They look around, nod, then close their eyes. After a few minutes—she told us what to expect, but it still amazes me—I hear a whooshing and creaking off in the distance. When I turn toward the sound, I see it: a red brick and glass building flying down toward us, sailing through the air on its own steam.

M and I duck, but the people don't appear to be concerned, so we look up again and watch the building slow, hover over the cracked concrete of its landing spot, and settle with a groaning of metal and crunching of stone onto the ground. A small plume of dust rises. The doors swing open and we all stroll inside.

At first I'm content to watch the humans, see what goes on inside a library. The young women holding hands seem to know where they want to go, heading off into the aisles of books. The children slide book after book from their mother's bag into a slot in the counter, giggling. The elderly man says something to the woman behind the counter, and she writes something down for him and points him off in another direction.

M nudges me. I follow him to the counter, but before he can even say a word, her eyes light up and she asks us a million questions about where we're from.

"Oh," she says. "I'd heard something about that church, but I didn't think any of you were left."

I feel like I'm crumbling into pebbles.

She must be able to tell, because she quickly adds, "But that doesn't mean there aren't. That's why libraries exist, after all. To learn things you don't already know."

The woman is very kind, searching in her computer, showing us her monitor when lead after lead comes up empty. "There used to be a lot more research into these phenomena—alchemical testing was suspected, but it was never really clear who was behind it. Folks were studying it, universities and private institutions alike, but then everything just kind of dried up." She leans closer and lowers her voice. "Some people say it's a government coverup. But then, there are so many conspiracy theories, it's hard to know what to believe. But I can show you where to poke around; you might find something unexpected."

Clearly, we hadn't thought this through. Neither of us can read.

"Ah, yes," says M. He hesitates, then asks her to write down some of the words we'll be searching for. With our list and a point in the right direction, we head off into the shelves.

"We'll look for matching words," says M. "Then we'll take the books home and learn to read."

"Or ask Dolores to read them to us."

"No!" Then his voice softens. "Dolores and her mother are busy with their new lives. We'll find our kind again soon, and then we'll have our lives back too. Everyone's happy."

I try not to show surprise at the quick shift in tone. "Right," I say. "Everyone's happy." I just wish I knew what he was trying to hide from Dolores and Rose.

M and I scan the books in the aisle we were directed to, looking for similarities between what the woman wrote on our paper and what we see on the spines. Despite my doubts, we actually find some matches. When we're ready, I pile them on M's back and hold them steady while we go to check them out.

One step closer to finding the City of Dancing Gargoyles. I should feel happier than I do, I suppose. They probably won't be the gargoyles we knew—M and I barely made it this far, and we had help—but we'll get to know the new ones. Things will be fine; we'll feel right at home with our own kind. Of course we will.

And once we find our new home, I'm sure Dolores will visit.

I hope.

FROM: Joseph Evans
TO: Manfred Himmelblau
CC: Meena Gupta

Subject: In the City of Laughing Ghosts

Location: Valley of Fire (former national park)

Shiver-cold wisps of mirth ply the air like sailboats above me. Sun bakes my skin, and I tilt my head back for the freshness of ghosts flitting overhead. Gauzy, ethereal gumdrops, they float just high enough for their spectral hems to graze my cheeks.

Laughter sinks from them like heavy soap bubbles, tiny plashes on my forehead, my arms, my chest. At first I wipe the shimmering residue away, but the ghosts are so happy, I give up. I'll shower back at the hotel.

Why are you so happy? I ask.

Silence, they tell me, and I feel the shame of the silenced.

But then they say
No, it is because of silence that we are happy.
We are free from husbands telling us what to do, and what they will do to us if we don't.
Free from what they did to us anyway.

We are free from commanders barking orders and marching us into war.
Free from the crack of a pistol when we turn to run for home.

We are free from the blood on our skin and the smoke in our throats and the screaming missiles and the rat-tatting machine guns and the thwopping rotors and the cries of hungry babies.
The babies are now silent.

Free at last, the ghosts croon in my head, dancing in sunshine, laughing their silent wet sparkles.

I twirl with them so they won't see me shake.

FROM: Meena Gupta
TO: Manfred Himmelblau

Subject: At Wit's End

Manfred, all I saw in the Valley of Fire were dust devils. Literally, nothing but sand twirling in the wind. Then out of nowhere, he started typing.

Please, do something. Arrange a call, talk to him.

Something's got to give.

XV.

The holster is heavy on my hips. It's overkill for the pistol Ben brought for me to practice with, but he thought I'd like it. He's not wrong. I rub my finger over its beechnut leather, gone soft and buttery with age, surprised at how much I love the velvety feel of it.

"All right, show me your stance," Ben says, standing to the side and behind me.

I shake out my arms and stand with my legs apart, steady but relaxed, knees slightly bent. It's bright out, but I'm wearing sunglasses and the cowboy hat he brought along—to set the mood, he said, like playacting would make me less nervous about shooting for the first time. I exhale, my heart pumping a bit faster as I grip the pistol high and tight like he told me.

"Good. Now draw, just like before."

Except it's not just like before. This time, the gun's loaded.

I take another deep breath before I pull the pistol out of the holster and hold it up in front of me, bringing my other hand up to meet it. Firm grip, straight line forearm to barrel, left hand slightly tilted down for maximum contact between palm and grip.

Ben circles behind me to see both sides. His voice is calm, encouraging: "Okay, make sure you're seeing your sights."

I focus down the sights, aiming for the cactus we've picked out.

"When you're ready: breathe out, steady, press."

I've watched him shoot several cacti already, each one fizzling and deflating like a balloon before pumping itself back up to its full, prickly plumpness. I still have a hard time thinking about shooting one.

"When you're ready," he repeats.

"Are there really no paper targets we can use? Bottles? Cans? Bad tippers?"

Ben laughs and I lower the gun.

"If you're going to defend yourself, you have to be prepared for the possibility of hurting someone."

"I'll shoot for the leg." I repeat the steps of raising my arms, settling my grip, sighting. Breathe out, concentrate. I press the trigger and clench my teeth at the recoil—I knew it was coming, but there's no way to prepare for the first kick, I suppose.

A puff of sand explodes to the side of the cactus. He doesn't even have to egg me on; I want to hit it now. I aim again, and the bullet whizzes right past the cactus.

"Higher," Ben says. "Give yourself a bigger target."

He means the heart of it, the nexus where arms branch out from the main stalk. He means shoot to kill. I tell myself it's just a cactus and squeeze the trigger. The cactus shudders and sways, air leaking out of a hole in one of its arms. It must just be a nick, because it's taking its time to deflate.

Ben claps as the cactus sputters to the ground. I lower the pistol, a little shake in my hand. But a minute later, he encourages me to try again, pointing out another target. I hit the cactus right in the meat on the second try. While it struggles up again, he points out another target, and I hit it. I'm aiming to kill.

I reholster the pistol, feeling lightheaded.

"It's more tiring than it seems, especially at first," he says. "You get used to it."

But do I want to get used to it? I wonder. In another couple of months, I could buy this gun. I'd have enough money. Then maybe a phone—a cheap one. But then, it's the same thing Mama says about bullets: maybe you can get the gun or the phone, but bullets and cell service are what adds up. And who have I got to call, anyway?

"What?" Ben asks.

I look up at him, and I'm not sure how long he's been watching me stare at nothing. "Oh, just going over the steps in my head again."

His dimples deepen with his cute little crooked-tooth smile. "You're hooked. I knew you'd be. Want another crack at it?" He points to the cactus I just shot, which is almost fully upright again.

"I'm good for the moment. We should be getting back anyway." I unbuckle the holster and hand it back to him.

"We can come out again when I'm back."

I nod. He's heading out of town for his side business—I guess Lake Security pay doesn't cut it on its own. But he won't say exactly where or for how long. At least I can stop lying to Mama for a bit, stop saying I'm out searching with E and M for their city when I'm actually with Ben. Trouble is, she's always here in my head with me, no matter how far I go.

While he stows our gear in his truck, I walk up to the last cactus I shot, now fully inflated again. I can see where the bullet went in, a slight pucker of a scar on tough, green skin. I stick a finger between the spines to see what it feels like, but before I can touch it, the scar pulls into itself and the cactus leans slightly away from me.

Ben puts a gentle hand on my shoulder, steering me away from the cactus, toward him. "Don't mind that. It's just a reflex." He encircles me in his arms, grinning. "I'll make you a gunslinger yet."

I scoff, and he kisses me, then his expression turns a little more serious.

"Look," he says. "Choice is up to you. Do you want to be vulnerable, like them?" He nods toward the cacti. "Or do you want to be safe? In charge?"

He takes both my shoulders in his hands. "I'm serious, Dolores. There are some bad people out there. You need to be smart."

His deep brown eyes are staring right into mine, and I feel like he's sincere, not just some gun-obsessed wacko. He seems to be truly concerned for me.

He tips my hat farther back on my head and leans in for a long, slow kiss. A little moan escapes his throat, and I melt. The hat tumbles to the ground and stays there while we get lost in each other for the next few minutes.

"Want to go somewhere more comfortable?" he asks, his voice soft and low. He trails his fingertips down my neck, and I imagine us somewhere shady and cool, away from the endless grit of sand. I imagine him sliding his palms down my back, the feel of his hands on my skin.

He brushes his lips against my neck, and I bury my fingers in his dark curls. His kisses turn into tiny bites, and his grip around me tightens. He moans again, more intensely, and I start to get a little nervous because it all feels like it's going too fast.

I pull back. "Maybe… when you get back."

A flash of anger passes over his face, and although he squelches it quickly, it's still frightening. I'm out here in the middle of nowhere with someone I don't really know that well. Someone armed.

He takes a deep breath and strokes my face with a finger. It looks like he's about to say something, but then he simply smiles and bends to pick up the hat. "Let's get you home," he says, placing it back on my head.

He opens the door for me, and I climb into his truck. He's fine now, if a little quiet, holding my hand as he drives—not dangerous, just disappointed. And now things feel awkward, just as he's going away for who knows how long.

What if he's undercover somewhere? What if he doesn't come back?

Sagebrush whips by my window as we head back to Carson City. I squeeze Ben's hand, missing him already.

FROM: Meena Gupta
TO: Manfred Himmelblau

Subject: In the City of Smiling Slippers

Location: Mead Pond (formerly Lake Mead), Nevada

It's cozy here in the City of Smiling Slippers. Anywhere you go, there's bound to be an armchair or a couch where you can sit back with a cup of cocoa and put your feet up and smile at the slippers smiling back at you.

They give you the slippers when you arrive, white with the classic yellow smiley-face, cheerful and familiar. There's a hearth on every block with a roaring fire, and the city hands out earbuds so you can listen to your favorite music. Everyone is wearing their robe, or at least sweats, and the air smells like pancakes and bacon in the morning, and barbeque in the afternoon, and chocolate at night.

Joseph I had been traveling for so long, it was the perfect place to slow down. We'd only meant to stay for a day or two, but somehow days turned into a whole week as we explored the streets with our cocoa, browsing bookstores and music stores, watching local artisans blow glass and weave baskets. We washed all our clothes, but were in no rush to put them back on—how often do you get the chance to spend the day in a robe?

We liked hanging out at the animal shelter, wiggling our toes in our smiling slippers every time a puppy or kitten went to a new forever home. We mulled over new shoes—despite the car, we've been doing a fair amount of walking—and gradually sampled every flavor in the ice cream shop, analyzing our slippers. We could have sworn their smiles got broader every time we found a new favorite flavor (yes, both of us, not just Joseph). And all this while eating mountains of pancakes and hamburgers and ribs, followed by pudding or cake or mousse every night.

I'd just curled into one corner of a couch under a shade tree with a new novel when Joseph, sitting on the other end, pulled our research notes out of his daypack. We'd spent many a morning this way, handing the binder back and forth, strategizing the next phase of our journey—and for once he wasn't just picking the most depressing places. It seemed like he was regaining his equilibrium. Yet that day my stomach tightened as he thumbed through the pages, unbending dogears on places we'd been while folding new ones on places yet to go.

"We don't have to decide right now, do we?" I asked.

He said there wasn't really anything left to document here and reminded me it was my turn to file. And he was right. I'd collected all the data we needed, and had started—but not finished—my report. I couldn't, however, find the will to file and move on. Joseph had stabilized so well here. And furthermore, it was all so…comfortable.

I convinced him to come look at the puppies one more time, thinking I might persuade him to foster one so we could stay a little longer. As we walked, he spilled a drop of cocoa on his right slipper, and the strangest thing happened: the smiley face on the slipper *licked its lips*, removing the stain, and winked.

Joseph and I looked at each other, dumbstruck.

"What just happened?" he whispered.

I dipped my finger in my cocoa and let a drop fall onto his left slipper.

That one also licked its lips, then closed both eyes in what looked like a moment of savoring. Both slippers' smiles grew even bigger.

He dropped his cocoa and kicked off his slippers, and as soon as they were off his feet my heart sank. There was no way he'd stay now.

It was all I could do to keep him from ripping his robe off right there in the middle of the street. I told him people were looking at us, I pleaded with him not to be the rude visitor, passing judgment on other cultures. Passersby maintained polite smiles and quickly looked away, as though embarrassed for us. Even the curve of their slippers' smiles seemed a little less generous now. A little less enthusiastic.

He noticed this too, but instead of trying to be happier again, he tightened his robe with a yank of the belt and turned, barefoot, back in the direction of our B&B.

"Oh, no you don't!" I shouted, picking up one of his slippers. "You don't get to just leave your shit all over."

I threw the slipper at him, and it bounced off his back. He turned, and I picked up the other slipper and threw it at him as well, which he caught but then dropped like it was on fire. I pointed down at both of them by his feet. "Those belong to the B&B. I don't care if you don't want to wear them, but you can't just dump them."

He simply stared at me with an impassive expression, further stoking my anger.

"Don't be such a baby, just put them in your pockets if you're too *scared* to wear them. Seriously, after all the messed-up places you dragged me to, *this* is what freaks you out?"

For a moment I felt bad. That last part wasn't exactly fair, because he wasn't the one who came up with the list of cities. But then I thought about how he'd targeted all the most harrowing places, so I went on:

"Mr. Root-for-the-Robots, Mr. Moon-the-Blankets, Mr. Never-Met-an-Ottoman-He-Didn't-Like!" I thought back to other moments I'd wished I were traveling with someone else. "I can't believe you actually ate one of those chocolates. It was looking right at you!" (I noticed he didn't mention that in the report, by the way.)

He'd finally heard enough, scowling at me while he snatched his slippers off the ground, stuffed them into a pocket, and marched back to the bed and breakfast.

At least, I assume he went straight there. I have no idea because I spent the day wandering the city, working my way up a flower-dotted hillside to the winery on top before adopting a bunny on my way back to the B&B late that afternoon. That's when Mr. Fluffers and I found out that Joseph had checked out of his room AND TAKEN THE CAR and left. He also had our research binder.

My slippers closed their eyes, and their idyllic smiles were the very embodiment of the peace I felt inside.

I worked out a monthly rate with the owners of the B&B, but I think they were more influenced by my slippers' beatific expression than my powers of negotiation. I think they see me as a good luck charm, and I'm happy to play the role of satisfied guest for everyone who visits. Because the thing is, it's not just a role. I truly am satisfied. Why would I not be, relaxing in my robe in the City of Smiling Slippers, drinking hot chocolate and sharing a room with Mr. Fluffers?

Do I sometimes wish Joseph hadn't taken the binder with all of our notes? Do I sometimes wonder what else is out there? Yes.

Don't misunderstand, this is not me quitting. Soon enough, I'll start again, visiting places on my own. On foot (thanks, Joseph).

When my smiling slippers open their eyes, I'll know it's time to begin again.

XVI.

M and I aren't making any headway with these books. I try another one, flipping it open and scanning the lines of symbols filling the pages top to bottom. Sometimes the books have pictures, photos or drawings; we've seen images of robots with swords, vine-covered cities, flying fences, statues on rafts, but no sign of gargoyles. I look over at M, holding another tome open against the floor with his paws and guessing at words under his breath.

M's been hoarding the books up in our belltower, for our eyes only. I'm grateful for this space, but as comforting as it is to live in a church again, there is no actual bell in this belltower, no ornamentation, no other gargoyles for company. To be honest, sometimes even M is too grumpy to be good company, preoccupied with finding our city.

And I can only spend so much time up here poring over books.

I climb down from the spire and head to the café. Dolores is alone folding cutlery into napkins when I arrive. Not with *him*, for once. She says "Hey" and fetches a bowl of water for me before sitting down with a glass for herself.

"Any luck?" she asks, reaching for another knife, fork, and spoon, rolling them into a napkin.

I shake my head. "I've got to find some way to sneak one of them out for you to read."

"Fat chance," she mutters. "M never sleeps."

I sigh and lean down to take a sip, but stop when I notice a reddish-brown stick floating in the water.

"It's cinnamon," says Dolores. "Try it."

I sniff. "It smells nice."

"Try it. I mean, don't eat it. Just drink."

The water seeps into my stone with a pleasant bit of warmth.

"Don't tell my boss," she whispers. "It's super expensive."

Well, it's clear why she's feeling magnanimous: she and Rose finally have a place to stay and all the food they need. She has a boyfriend, despite her mother's wishes. She's even saving up a little stash of money her mother doesn't know about—another secret I have to keep for her. But she's happy, for now.

"Anyway," she says, "I've been asking around, but so far no one knows anything about a city of gargoyles, dancing or otherwise. But there's another place you might try."

I finish my bowl of water. She pushes a chair back from the table for me, and I climb onto it to face her more easily.

"There's another library—"

I scoff.

"Hear me out: you don't need to read these books. They talk. It's called the City of Fretting Books."

"Fretting? Isn't that bad?"

She shrugs. "Not necessarily. Mama certainly fits that description, and it's annoying, but it means she's prepared for just about anything. It's only a few days away from here. You should be able to get there and back on a good solid soak and a canteen each."

"Sounds promising. But what should I tell M? How am I supposed to have found out about this City of Fretting Books?" Dolores knows as well as I do that M doesn't want anyone else snooping into his business.

"We'll figure something out," she says. Then she sighs and fiddles with a fork. "Look… I'm sorry I asked you to lie for me. I mean, of course she knows everything. She busted me last time I snuck out with him."

"How? I didn't say anything."

"I know. I'll bet it was M. He never liked Ben—Mama doesn't either." She twists her lips. "And you don't either. But you helped me anyway."

I hold my tongue. I understand that she finds him charming, but Rose is skeptical about him and his "side business," and her instincts are usually good. It would be easier if he simply didn't return.

"I shouldn't have put you in that situation to begin with," Dolores says. "I should have just been honest."

"Yes."

She waits for a moment, like she's expecting me to go on. "Yeah, okay," she says, slapping my front leg. "This is the part where you accept my apology."

"Apology accepted." I can't help but smile, and we laugh.

I should be asking for directions now, reporting back to M, preparing for our journey. But instead I sit, and she tells me about other people she's met since we last spoke, and we both lean forward as she whispers how much in tips she's added to her little "freedom stash" as she calls it.

"Mama's talking like we might stay here for a while," she says. "Says she might take some classes to learn accounting or something to get a better job. Says I should start thinking about college?" She shakes her head with a small smile. "It's wild to think about the future."

I can't complain either. This isn't the worst city to be stuck in, or the worst human to be stuck with.

From time to time, it even rains.

FROM: Manfred Himmelblau
TO: Meena Gupta

FW: In the City of Shrinking Jellyfish

The latest from Joseph

------------Forwarded Message-------------
FROM: Joseph Evans
TO: Manfred Himmelblau

Subject: In the City of Shrinking Jellyfish

Location: perhaps everywhere

We were leviathans once. We floated down the streets of our oceanic city, swallowing immensities of krill, laughing, talking, visiting our mothers, mating—just like any other civilization. Fish glided among us, and lobsters pulsed through our ranks, propelled by their twitching tails. The crabs always amused us when they paddled by, furiously waving their legs for locomotion. Everyone had somewhere to be, something important to do. Our lone predators were the sharks, but they could only hunt us in shivers, so we developed an early warning system to alert us if they approached en masse.

Perhaps by now you feel a slight twinge of recognition, the ghost of a legend pulsing at memory's edge, triggered by the word "leviathan." But we digress...

We still aren't certain what triggered the change—although we have our ideas. At first we remarked to each other how oddly powerful the ocean currents seemed of late. Then we shared an uncanny feeling that the reefs of our city loomed larger around us than ever before. *Was someone doing construction,* we wondered.

We began getting lost on our way to work, but we didn't criticize one another for being late, because we all suffered similar disorientation.

No one wanted to face it, so for many years we simply avoided the topic, even as our fish and crustacean neighbors grew to match, then surpass us, in size. In some misguided attempt at magical thinking, we ignored what was happening until one of us was eaten by a shark—a single shark. Then we couldn't deny it anymore: we'd been shrinking.

Our thriving society has by now been diminished to a delicate flutter of nerves. Once we swam in magnificent, diaphanous undulations; now we squirt about in anxious spurts. A group of us was once called a flotilla; now we're called a smack. The indignity.

It's no wonder we developed a sting.

But we're done being slight and slighted. Our scientists—yes, we're small, but we're not stupid—have developed alternatives. Every species on the earth, they say, has been affected by changing environments. From air, to soil, to sea, the chemical composition of every organism's home has been altered. But you humans have been so busy watching the canary in the coalmine, you completely missed us slipping into smallness in the sea.

Our scientists tell us we can use our undetected change to our advantage, immersing ourselves in the problem, putting on the armor of our enemy—to be blunt, inhabiting the cities of humans, now that they have taken our cities from us.

If we all work together, they say, we jellies could rule the world.

We could shrink further and bury ourselves in miles of silt, collapse the food chain, starve humans out of existence, then resurface and bloom back into a fresh new world.

We could become light enough to evaporate into the clouds, then rain down onto the cities and sting human flesh until it rots away.

We could even go microscopic and embed ourselves in fish, then the people who eat them, then wriggle through their bloodstreams into their brains and kill them.

Or perhaps, instead of killing them, we could use our filament tentacles to redirect their synaptic connections. They wouldn't even know we were there, and we'd multiply and prosper. Our offspring would completely inhabit the human bodies, and live in their cities, which would now be ours as well. And the humans wouldn't be any the wiser.

You hoped, perhaps, that our scientists' theories would be about how to reverse the change, grow back to our original glorious size, and live in peace?

Well, so did we.

You hoped, perhaps, that there was some other choice?

Yes, so did we.

But there is no other choice. You haven't left us one. In fact, you've left us with only one way to go: in.

And perhaps we're already there.

FROM: Meena Gupta
TO: Manfred Himmelblau

Subject: Question

Hi Manfred. I got your email from Joseph. I'm still in the City of Smiling Slippers, but I promise I won't stay here forever. I'll catch up to him and start reporting again soon. I know it's important to keep documenting. I haven't forgotten what we need to talk about when I get back. I just needed a break.

I forgot to ask: a young woman I met on a previous trip emailed to ask me if we knew anything about a City of Dancing Gargoyles. I didn't see anything in the manual. I remember when I met them, they said gargoyles were coming after them, but I didn't see any.

Do you know anything about this?

Thanks in advance,

Meena

XVII.

As we suspected, the City of Fretting Books turned out to be useless. But we were able to pick up on another lead there—book people know book people—which has now brought us to the City of Bleeding Books.

Bleeding books certainly sound more serious.

But will they tell us what we want to know?

We stand before a rocky incline, looking at the entrance to a cave about ten feet up. The entrance looms black against the brightness of day. We climb over crumbling, sand-colored rocks to reach the entrance. Cool air wafts out from the cave, carrying a copper-tinged scent and strange, wet sounds. Sliding, flapping—of pages, I assume. I hope. Heavy sighing emanates from the cave as well. Once in a while, a sob.

If I had blood or veins, they would be running a little colder now.

M's expression sets in determination, and he pads inside. I follow, stepping forward cautiously while my eyes adjust to the gloom.

The first thing I notice, aside from the increased intensity of the metallic smell, is that the floors are sticky. I lift my tail, shuddering.

M moves away from me, toward torchlit figures standing in endless rows of shelves. His head is down. He's scenting.

I follow him between shelves full of dripping books, maneuvering around lumpy, wet piles of pages that have fallen to the floor. In every aisle, at least one person stands, sifting through books that barely hold together, sorting and re-sorting the pages. Someone's crying.

"How are we supposed to find anything here?" I whisper.

M stops in a cross-aisle between the ends of bookshelves and sniffs to the left and right. "Everything is here. This is where they assemble history. It could be past or present history. Or potential history—history of the future." He sniffs to the left again before heading in that direction and turning into another aisle.

"But how will we find the City of Dancing Gargoyles?" I ask. The smell is almost unbearable. My foot slips on the slime. "And which past will it be in?"

M sniffs down one aisle after another while I tiptoe along behind him trying to keep as clean as I can. Finally he stops and addresses a man placing a relatively intact book on a shelf.

"What are you working on here?" he asks.

The man startles.

"We mean you no harm," I say.

He shakes his head, hand on his chest. "Individually, no. But when you find your city, you will pose a grave danger."

Bewildered, I look at M—who seems unfazed.

"What city?" M demands.

The man backs away, eyes wide.

"M," I ask. "What's going on?"

"Come, be reasonable," M purrs, stalking toward him. "It's just a story. You don't believe everything you read, do you?"

The man stares at M, shaking. He turns to flee, but M is too quick: with a roar, he leaps and knocks the man down in the aisle.

"Where is it?" M growls into his face. "Where is our city?"

I hiss at M to stop, afraid the whole library will descend upon us. But despite all the scuffling and knocking as M pins the man to the floor, no one comes to his aid.

The man squirms under M's grip, too terrified to call out. The more M noses around his head and neck, the quieter the man becomes. I can hear him struggling to breathe with M sprawled on top of him.

"M!" I hiss again. "What's going on?"

Slowly, M lolls his tongue out of his mouth and licks the man's cheek, clearing it of blood. Both the man and I are immobilized.

"Please, M. Don't do this."

M shifts and I rush forward, but instead of attacking, M is letting the man go. He scrambles to his feet and runs away in a panic, slipping twice on the bloody floor before turning a corner out of sight. His footsteps splat away against the ambient flap and shuffle of wet pages.

M's face is the picture of satisfaction, his muzzle and paws soaked in blood. "I know how to get to our city. I've got its scent."

"What did you do to him?" I look down at my own bloody feet and back at M.

"Don't look at me like that," he scoffs. "You were willing to live off their corpses."

Suddenly it seems like all the moisture has left my body. I'd forgotten all about my "backup plan" in the desert, if Dolores and her mother hadn't survived.

"What was it you called them?" he says. "'Walking canteens'?"

My chest feels like it's cracking. "It's not like that anymore."

He smirks and huffs out a breath. "Well, you don't have to worry about her anymore. She's safe now."

"What does that mean?"

"The young man, the one you and Rose were so worried about. Ben. He won't be back."

I cock my head and wait for him to explain.

"Your instincts were right: yours, Rose's, even Dolores' before her hormones overrode them. He would have brought more trouble into her life. But now he won't be a problem; ergo, no worries about Dolores; ergo, we can go."

I narrow my eyes at him. "What did you do?"

M merely shakes his mane, then brushes against me on the way to the exit. "We have an opportunity to make this a better world, E. Don't you want that?"

FROM: Manfred Himmelblau
TO: Meena Gupta

Subject: In the City of Wrestling Kudzu

Transcription of voicemail received from Joseph's phone—NOT Joseph's voice—check your voicemail for forwarded message.

Location: Unknown (this one isn't on our list. We think the call came from somewhere back near Tonopah)

I've arranged a car for you. You'll see why.

I am hoping things are not really as dire as they sound.

I am aware that my neighbors would rather I had not been true to my nature, had not been myself, had not—been. I know that people would much prefer their homes free of my creeping vines, that they wish I hadn't choked the life out of their tomato plants or twined up the stalks of their prize rosebushes and strangled them cold. I realize that every tree I kill decreases the value not only of the house next to it, but, slowly, of the whole neighborhood as well.

And yet, you've come to see me. You stand there and goggle at the "havoc" I've wreaked. That's what you visitors call it: havoc. Destruction. Desolation.

I call it survival.

[rustling, like something moving through leaves]

You should know that I've tried, really tried, to understand why I do what I do, why I was never content to climb up just one telephone pole, but instead felt compelled to overtake every stop sign, billboard, railing, and power line in town. Don't you think I've asked myself when enough will be enough? After all, by the time people noticed me, I owned much more land than anyone else in the city. By that measure I was the richest...*entity* in town.

And perhaps that pause was part of the problem, because one wants to say the richest *person* in town, doesn't one? But I am, of course, not a person. I've grown all over the possessions of people, their homes and the fences surrounding them, their yards, their trellises intended for other things, their derelict bicycles, lost frisbees, deflated soccer balls, rusted-out trucks, losing lottery tickets, empty soda cans, dropped pacifiers, discarded condoms, lost socks. My tendrils clasp onto these things, my gorgeous green leaves caressing everything a person could ever desire, and yet I am not a person myself.

[more rustling of leaves]

It's no use shaking your head. I hold no illusions on where I stand with you humans. Your kind has made that abundantly clear by the way you've cut into me, slicing away at my stalks and pulling me down from my path toward sunlight. The people who used to live here made a valiant effort for many years, but eventually most of them gave up, packed everything I didn't already possess, and left. Every time another house went empty, I should have been glad for another victory. But something pulled at me almost as powerfully as the hands that tried to tug me away from the lightposts along the bike trail. I felt...empty. Despite everything in my grasp, I was lonely. Unfulfilled. I thought I missed people. I thought I wanted to live amongst them and perhaps, if I could change my nature, be accepted by them.

[more rustling]

Careful, watch where you're stepping. I'm everywhere.

And so I turned my attention especially to those few people who had stayed on. I tried to fight my own instincts and not strangle their cars, or their pets, or their gardens. And for a while, I was able to (largely) contain myself—after all, I had all the surrounding undeveloped area to conquer.

Despite the mental stimulation my experiment with restraint provided, my dominant state became one of lassitude only intermittently marked by a spark of purpose. After a season of languor, I finally recognized the pattern: it was only during moments of struggle, when one of the residents tried to pull me away from their front door or pry the family dog from my grasping tendrils, that I felt alive. Those flashes of opposition invigorated me, made me feel like there was something more to life than merely drinking in water and sunlight. I'd discovered my purpose. I'd missed the fight!

[rustling and a thump, followed by more rustling]

You're all right. You tripped over me while backing up, but I caught you before you fell.

But where was I? Yes, I'd missed the give and take of growth and battle, that tug of war for every inch of space I occupied. It was no fun spreading out along the countryside, unopposed. I felt most alive when I had to connive and wrestle for a place to unfurl each new leaf. Winning something, I found, makes possession all the sweeter.

[rustling and grunting]

I'll let you go in a moment, I'm just making sure you're not hurt.

And so, I was back to my old ways, and though the pets ran like cowards, the humans put up a fight. They hacked away at me, poisoned me, even tried to burn me out, though I grow so quickly there's no sign of those battles anymore. It was a glorious year, but I'll admit, at the end I was too aggressive.

You're shaking now. I'm sorry to frighten you.

That's my weakness, I suppose: I'm too aggressive. That's why I have to keep enticing people to visit the City of Wrestling Kudzu. Tourists come, walk around and gawk, then when I get the sense they're about to go I'll grab one of them, give them a little scare, share a bit of nervous energy in the tussle before I let them extract their leg and drive off to visit the world's largest ball of twine or wherever they go next. People usually come in groups, not alone like you, so they know no one's *really* in danger. Not really. I mean, they always know someone could go for help if things got out of control, so it's harmless. Mostly.

It's just that sometimes I can't seem to figure out when to stop. And I must say you're not making it easy for me.

[rustling and a muffled yell, like someone gagged]

Please stop wriggling. I just told you that fighting is what excites me, what drives me to keep twining and growing and surrounding. What causes me to squeeze and smother. To hold forever.

Please be still. Stop fighting. It's in your best interests to just relax and breathe.

Can't you be still?

I'm begging you, please be still!

[rustling]

[pause]

Oh dear.

It's happened again.

[pause]

I'm so lonely.

[END OF CALL]

FROM: Meena Gupta
TO: Manfred Himmelblau

RE: In the City of Wrestling Kudzu

Got it. I'll find him. I'll keep filing from the road.

Meanwhile, any news on that other city, the one with the gargoyles?

Thx.

Meena

XVIII.

Today is the day. M and I climb out of the fountain in front of our church, thoroughly soaked, and strap two canteens each around our necks. We have a long journey ahead of us, although I don't know exactly how long it will be—the downside of being fully saturated is that we're now too heavy for M to fly and carry me at the same time. We'll have to walk.

"Are you sure two canteens will be enough?" I ask.

"More excuses?"

"I'm just concerned—"

"If you don't want to go—"

"I didn't say that."

He sighs and sits, like he's trying to listen, but I know he's ready to spring back up again as soon as I relent. "Don't you want to go home?" he asks.

He keeps telling me, *where there are gargoyles, there is home*. Maybe. But there's water and company *here*, and we've never been *there*, and he doesn't even know exactly where *there* is.

"We could at least wait until Dolores finds out what it's really called."

He frowns at me. "It's called the City of Dancing Gargoyles, and it doesn't concern her at all."

"You were happy enough to take her help finding it."

We're busy glaring at one another when Dolores jogs up to us.

"There you are. You weren't going to leave without saying goodbye, were you?"

"No, of course not. We were about to come see you, right M?"

"Yes, of course," he says, barely disguising his eagerness to be on our way.

"Thank you again for the waterblankets," I say. The cloths are folded and strapped to M's back. They're an especially considerate farewell gift, able to distill moisture directly out of the air.

"They have everything in Carson City," she says. "If you can get a merchant to stop crying long enough to sell it to you."

I smile despite how I feel. I'm going to miss her.

"How long did you say it'll take?" she asks, breaking the silence.

"We'll be fine," M assures her.

"Sure, sure… You're heading what direction again?"

I gesture in the direction M told me, to his visible annoyance.

"Isn't that right into the desert?" Dolores asks.

M heaves a great sigh and stands up again. "We really must be going."

"I just mean..." Dolores fidgets. "I mean, how much do you know about this place? What if it's dangerous? I'm just saying maybe you should wait until Meena gets—"

"Who, or what, is *Meena*," sniffs M. "And why should I care what it says?"

"*She's* a researcher, and she studies these cities, everything that's happened since the Testing, and—"

M interrupts again. "And what exactly does she know about the City of Dancing Gargoyles?"

"Well, she doesn't have the details yet; she's waiting for more information from Manfred."

"And who is this *Manfred* now?" M shakes his mane in frustration. "Honestly, E, it sounds like she's making up excuses for us not to go, which is sweet, but—"

"I am not!"

"So, if you wish us well, we should be on our way. E."

I hesitate, looking back and forth between M and Dolores.

"What E seems to be forgetting," M says, "is that we gargoyles are truly communal creatures, built of and related by stone. Even after we were able to move and think for ourselves, we found we needed one another."

Dolores looks at me and I confirm with a nod.

M continues: "Everyone from our church was made of the same stone, so we could tell by their coloring who was healthy, and who needed help. If someone needed moisture, we could share ours with them. By contact. And we did it willingly—"

"Until we didn't," I interject.

"True. When things got bad, very bad, each of us began to think only of our own individual benefit. Except E and I. We stuck together. And now that we've found more of our kind," M says training his gaze on me, "we should be among them."

Dolores looks so sad I can barely stand it. "Can't you stay just a little longer?" she asks. "Till I hear back from Meena? I'll go to the library and check my email right now."

But M is ready to go. And I can't let him do this on his own.

"Well," she sighs. "Here's something for the road." She unscrews the lid of one of my canteens and drops a stick of cinnamon inside before sealing it back up and enveloping me in a hug. Now I feel like the farthest thing in the world from stone.

"Be careful," she says, her arms still around me. "Write sometimes, or whatever gargoyles do." She lets me go and looks me in the eyes. "I'll miss you."

I can't speak, so I nod and flash a smile.

She offers a cinnamon stick to M, but he shakes his head.

"As you like," she says, a bit of frost in her voice. "Be safe, and take care of E, okay? I hope you find what you're looking for."

M and I head out. Every time I turn to look back, she waves.

"Stay focused," M snaps. "Stop worrying about her. She's safe with her mother. That boy Ben won't come back."

"Will you finally tell me what you did to him?"

"Forget him. Forget Dolores and Rose, forget Carson City and cinnamon sticks," he snorts. "We've got more important matters ahead."

I look back one more time. Dolores is gone.

FROM: Manfred Himmelblau
TO: Meena Gupta

Subject: The City of Dancing Gargoyles

Any sign of Joseph?

I received a puzzling voice message that may wind up being of interest to your friend searching for this gargoyle city. The message is quite bizarre, though, and a bit alarming, so I want to confirm the source before I forward it to you. I do not want to propagate a false accounting or give credence to a prank.

Even if I confirm the source, I fear it may not be reliable—as you know, the archives in the City of Bleeding Books are notoriously subjective, and I may not be able to vouch for the information.

I will inform you as soon as possible.

Please send news of Joseph.

FROM: Meena Gupta
TO: Manfred Himmelblau

Subject: Search Update/Report: In the City of Sneaking Needles

Location: Goldfield, Nevada

I think Joseph is okay. I haven't seen him, but I spoke to a waitress who said he came through here yesterday. He didn't say where he was heading. Aside from ordering, she said, the only person he spoke to was himself... But he's still alive at least, and well enough to travel.

Meanwhile, here's my report

Transcript of interview with Thomas Irving (TI), metallurgical biologist

MG: I'm speaking with Thomas Irving, a metallurgical biologist from Goldfield, Nevada. He's part of a team traveling in a steel reinforced SUV to New Winchester, Nevada, the City of Sneaking Needles. My first question is, of course, why.

TI: Why, indeed. Why would anyone want to visit the City of Sneaking Needles, a place where at any time you might get pricked from behind, turn, and see nothing? These needles aren't wielded by anyone—they simply are. At a time and in a world where we crave explanations, these needles simply are. No one wants to go to the City of Sneaking Needles—the inhabitants have all deserted it—but *we* must, because we study the needles. They're spreading, so we must go to their city before they come to us.

MG: You say these needles are spreading?

TI: Yes, and it is terrible to imagine the kind of life in which, at any moment, from anywhere, a needle might come at you. It wouldn't matter where you were: at work, or at school, or out walking your dog, or having a picnic, or watching a movie, or having a drink, or attending a concert, or even sleeping in your own bed. The needle would stick you and disappear, and you'd never know why, never find out what you could have done to avoid it. Not even staying home would keep you safe. In fact, some of the most heartbreaking needlesticks have happened in the home—many even involving children. And there's no one to hold to account.

MG: But have there been any sightings in Goldfield yet?

TI: No, not yet in Goldfield proper. But the needles are tenacious, striking, darting, making their presence known, expanding their reach. We simply have no choice but to go there and study the phenomenon.

We need to know what causes it, and how we might avoid it, or even stop it altogether. Our community would ask no less of us—who wouldn't want to be safe? We must climb into our needle-proof metal suits and march into town, vigilant, wary, wondering when the next needle will strike, never knowing why, researching and recording, wondering what it must have been like before the whole town finally decided that this was no way to live, and left for good.

We're determined to keep the needles at bay, not only for our own people, but for the sake of those who have escaped and come to warn us. We're thankful for them, but especially for the first one who wondered how it would be to not have needles everywhere, who spoke to others about how it might feel to breathe and sit and walk and play and simply be without needles, who encouraged others to envision true freedom—to imagine an even more beautiful way of life.

XIX.

M and I walk nonstop for days, but not in the direction I expected. When M said we wouldn't go thirsty, I thought we'd turn north toward the rains after getting out of town, or loop west into the trees. But he keeps heading east into the desert. I'm grateful for the waterblankets from Dolores; turns out they deflect heat as well as retain moisture, which is crucial now that we're not stopping to rest even during the hottest part of the day.

I'm not exactly clear on where we're going, but M tells me I'll be delighted. The important thing, he says, is that there are more of our kind there, and no one dries up, and they will welcome us with open arms, wings, claws, and paws.

On the fourth or fifth day, M tells me we're close. I can't hear it yet, but he's the one with the keener ears.

As we walk, he glances over and eyes me appraisingly. "Are you nervous?"

It seems a little disloyal, feeling anything but joy at the prospect of meeting more gargoyles. And yet: "Yes."

"It's all right," he says. "I'm a bit anxious too. We've got a lot to catch up with."

"Catch up with?"

M takes a deep breath. "Yes. I haven't wanted to say anything because it's—well, I've only had a sense of it. I've been questioning myself to be honest. But the closer we get, the more certain I am it's true."

"Is this another one of your stories?"

"We're close, E, and we can make a difference. The gargoyles have gathered, and we can make the world a better place, but all of us are needed."

His tone is a bit feverish now. A bit unnerving.

"They've been gathering and practicing," he continues. "Learning the steps to a transformation that will lead to a new start. We can remake things, E, only this time we'll be in charge of our own fate."

I stop. "What are you talking about?"

M keeps going for a few steps before stopping as well. He turns to face me. "We were made by humans, but that's where our allegiance ends. For their good and ours, it has to. We're not wiping anyone out, we're making a new world right here on earth."

Even in the heat, something in his voice chills me. "What does that mean?"

"We can go back to how things once were, E, don't you want that? To go back to the way it was before humans ran amok, before machines and exhaust, before the grime that settled into our pores and dulled our gleam, before the fumes that cooked the planet and acidified the water and killed millions of defenseless species?"

"But—but they made us. And their Testing awakened us."

"And that can't be changed now. Nor should it be." He turns and continues walking.

I follow, stunned.

"Everywhere the Testing has happened," he explains, "our dancing has manifested. Have you wondered why the trees shoot, or why the wolves float, or why the bats binge?"

He's referring to stories he told us back at the church. Stories I thought were just tall tales, fables for our amusement. "What do you mean, M? What's going on?"

"This is why dinosaurs swear, and jellyfish shrink, and bonfires sing. They are all part of a dance that will heal the earth, one tiny bit at a time. They've all been dancing in their own way, and as their numbers have grown, so has their power."

"Come on, now, you sound—"

"Somewhere on a distant shore, statues danced an entire village to madness; somewhere out in the desert, robots danced a town into oblivion; in a city to the north, for just one second, magicians danced the entire planet into the sky. The butterflies have spoken. The birds have spilled their secrets into the wind, and the bats have—"

"M, stop!"

He does. He's still and silent, but instead of bringing relief, his silence just opens my ears to something else. A faint, rhythmic thumping, but not of a drum. It's harder, sharper. The sound of stone striking stone. Even from a distance, each beat resonates inside me.

Something changes in M's eyes: the color deepens, his stone darkening like it's damp. But gargoyles don't cry.

The darkening widens, radiating outward from his eyes, replacing his parched grey skin with an obsidian shine, until his entire body has the sheen of polished black marble shot through with brilliant white veins.

He nods at me, and I look down. My body has turned a vibrant green, accented with swirling bands of silver. I turn, and sunlight glints off my skin. I feel powerful, like I belong somewhere. Here. And not merely as ornamentation or afterthought, to be left behind, forgotten and crumbling. I feel like I was always meant to be. Like I'm significant. Like I deserve to *be*.

"This is how *gargoyles* dance," M says. "Isn't it wonderful to feel like this? Aren't you glad we came?"

I am. Yet something feels off. Perhaps I don't trust change that comes so quickly. "But… What are the trees doing, exactly, and the bonfires? What about the bees, or the bats? How are they helping?"

M just smiles and continues walking toward the sound. And I see it now, through the wavy haze of desert heat, shapes moving, hopping up and down. The City of Dancing Gargoyles.

Despite my doubts, I follow.

FROM: Meena Gupta
TO: Manfred Himmelblau

Subject: Search Update/Report: In the City of Warring Babies

I keep just missing him. But people have seen him—I guess he sticks out, which in a way is great, in terms of tracking him down, but...

I'm not far behind him, though. I'll catch up.

And thanks for the info on the gargoyle city. Sounds very—I'm not even sure what, like a cult. I thought only humans fell for those.

I'll forward it to my friend with a caution and MASSIVE caveats. It's so far into the desert, she won't be able to get there, anyway.

Here's my report on the City of Warring Babies:

Transcribed wording from a letter tacked to the door of a bungalow down the street from my inn (the baby in question was, in fact, quite loud)

Location: Verdi, Nevada

When you moved here, we all tried to tell you it's not your fault. Some babies just scream, and we know you've exhausted all possibilities because you've told us—exhausted—everything you've tried: every doctor's visit, all the cognitive tests and aromatherapy and audio therapy and teething rings and parent support groups and baby's first bloodwork and even your great-granny's poultice, just on a tiny patch, though, and only after testing it on yourself first, of course.

But nothing works: your baby won't stop screaming, and sometimes you almost feel like your baby's against you, like it hates you, and it won't stop wailing until it knows you're dead and buried.

Please know this is not at all true.

In this city, your baby's screeching has nothing to do with you. Your baby is at war with someone you don't even know: the baby down the street, or the one across town, or the one that was just born yesterday and is still in the hospital receiving its first instructions. All babies in this city are at war—which is not to say they are all warriors.

You might be tempted to assume that the most vocal babies, like yours, will be the fiercest, that they'll bring that brawling energy into whatever battles they face. You might also assume that not all of these battles will be literal, physical fights, because how many direct combat cultures are left in the world? Certainly not ours (on a good day).

So you're perfectly right, the vast majority of the wars your baby will wage will be figurative. They might face individual skirmishes (say, deciding whether or not to cheat on a test), or interpersonal conflicts (whether or not to let a friend cheat off of their test) or societal battles (whether to vote for candidate X or Y, or just run for office themselves and do all the cheating firsthand).

But your assumptions about modality are flawed. A riotous baby might become a courageous fighter, or it might reveal itself as the one who cries "uncle" before the real fight has even begun. A quiet baby might grow to run and hide, or it might mature into someone who will wait and see, studying how to insert a stealthy knife, planning just when and where to strike for maximum effect. This knife might be figurative or literal, and you might be pleased or chagrined, depending. There's no way to know yet, and nothing to be done.

The baby your baby is raging at might be screeching back at this very moment. Or it might be cooing to itself in delighted mockery. Or it might be lying perfectly still, calculating serenely, the only sound in the nursery the gentle sucking on its thumb, perhaps the tinkle of a windup mobile rotoring plushies in circles above its crib—not that the baby would know, because it's likely gazing up at a point beyond the fuzzy yellow whales swimming their lazy laps overhead, its eyes on a future coalescing in tune to your baby's screams, calmly choosing its weapons (money? knives? pride?), planning how to negotiate terms of engagement, and contemplating already how silently they will shatter, how smoothly the blade will slide through skin.

FROM: Manfred Himmelblau
TO: Meena Gupta

FWD: In the City of Stinking Hills

Another update from Joseph, another city unknown to us. IP address untraceable.

And I wouldn't underestimate gargoyles, Meena. I hope the information I sent you serves to deter your friend from seeking them out, at least until after we've had an opportunity to check things out. You did tell her we'd look into it first, yes?

After finding Joseph, of course.

------------Forwarded Message-------------

FROM: Joseph Evans
TO: Manfred Himmelblau

Subject: In the City of Stinking Hills

Letter of Invitation slipped under my hotel room door

Location Notes: You mustn't follow me here

Nothing ever really changes in the City of Stinking Hills, and yet, people keep on coming. Which means, sure, it's growing, but when you get right down to it, it's always more of the same. But I invite you all the same, for I've heard such cities interest you.

No matter when folks arrive, Mayor Rat is usually the first to greet them—yes, an actual four-footed, twitchy-nosed, naked-tailed, beady-eyed rat. To be clear, she's just honorary mayor, but some days I almost feel like she's more well-liked around here than our actual mayor: me.

No, we're not a garbage dump. That would be sad. We're just a city that stinks, hillwise, meaning each hill has a certain distinct aroma.

If you arrive by train, which most travelers do, you'll disembark on Smokebelch Ridge. It'll hit you like you're huffing ashtrays in the middle of a factory smokestack, but since you'll be here to visit me, you won't stay on that hill for very long.

Head west and you'll descend out of that stench and climb Dung Mountain next. Don't worry, it's not an actual mountain, but yes, it smells like actual dung. An old dairy farmer lives on top of that hill. Retired. Thought he'd never quit farming down in the valley, but Mother Nature made that decision for him one night when she sent a pack of wolves over to feast on the herd. Killed 'em all, directly or indirectly, either in the pandemonium or afterward from shock and broken legs and such. Poor man. Broke his heart so bad he couldn't even think about starting over, even after his sons moved him up to Dung Mountain temporarily, while they cleared out the wolves. Took 'em years, but they killed the alpha, then the next alpha, and the next, until the rest eventually wised up and took off. But by that time their father'd gotten comfortable up there on the hill, surrounded by the memory of caring for his herd, feeding and milking, mucking out the barn. Says he doesn't mind it up there on Dung Mountain, especially as his sons are close by. They live up the next hill, the one that smells of wet pelts and blood and viscera rotting in the sun.

You may feel like rushing off that hill, but don't say I didn't warn you about what comes next. You'll think you stepped inside an old closet full of fetid shoes. You're not far off, though the young widow who lives up there would simply shake her head and smile, and say a mite sheepishly, "Some people say there's a right powerful odor up here, but I don't smell a thing." Despite the tangy, overripe sock stink up on Sock Mountain, I believe her. I don't think she smells a thing. That's what love can do to you. Or grief. Whichever it is, she's happy as a clam up there with that last lingering bit of her husband to keep her company.

Now, I know I said we don't live on a dump (despite Mayor Rat), but I do own that there is a hill that smells a lot like one. The couple who lives on that hill used to be a greedy king and queen in another life. They hoarded food and demanded that lavish feasts be cooked and served for them and them alone. They weren't gluttons, though; they never attempted to eat it all. But they invited no one else to share, and ordered all of the leftovers thrown out. On more than one occasion they sacked a cook for trying to sneak food out of the palace, and considered themselves benevolent for not having anyone executed for the crime.

"The peasants didn't work hard enough," they'd say. "Maybe if they'd worked harder, they could've paid for their own feasts."

Well, the castle they live in now is even larger than the palace they had before. It stinks to high heaven and is plagued by flies, and unlike the widow on top of Sock Mountain, they smell every bit of it. Thing is, they won't give it up for anything. You'd think it's some cosmic form of punishment, but no, they moved there of their own free will. They'll never leave. They get to hold on, olfactorily, to each and every morsel they've never tasted. They're so greedy, they won't even give up the stench of their own excess.

You'll be walking at a good clip by then, I'm sure, and by comparison, Beer Hill may be a relief—until you get closer. You'll see a guy reclining in a La-Z-Boy at the top of the hill, watching TV. No house, just the guy in his recliner with a drink holder for his beer and the TV on a rickety stand. When you get close, though, you'll realize he's not really watching the game; he's staring into the middle distance thinking about something that seems to hold him in place. The moth-eaten letter jacket will be a clue. Glory days, as that song goes. And then the stink of stale beer and vomit will make sense.

After that hill you'll come to another one smelling of dog farts and skunk. You'll feel bad for everyone whistling and calling out "here boy," empty leashes swaying in their hands. But there's nothing you can do for them. Their dogs would never go to a stranger like you.

When you get to the following hill, you might wonder why the dogs haven't migrated there, with its stench of liverwurst and limburger cheese and pickling brine. But there's only a house with shuttered windows. No one has ever seen who lives there.

By that point, climbing all those hills in the heat, you might be worried you'll never find mine. You might be tempted to forget your visit and just head back. But don't worry, you'll find me. Everyone does. And you won't be able to turn back anyway.

There you'll be. I'll see you and wave. You might not be able to see me at first, but I'll see you, and I'll know by the way you'll lift your head when you detect the singular aroma of my hill. You'll just need to keep going, keep following that cloying scent. Its sweetness will surprise you; I'll see it in your expression even from a distance.

Of course, the closer you get, the sourer and more fecal the scent will become—but as I've told you, you won't be able to turn back. No matter how you twist and turn, your feet will no longer have the power to carry you in any other direction. Don't worry, I'll have you, and I'll bring you the rest of the way. You won't be lonely: everyone winds up here eventually. I won't say you'll like it up here in my cool, dark house, but you won't hate it either. You won't feel anything either way in my stately old manse on top of Corpse Hill.

My arms aren't the softest, having lost all their flesh, but I will open them wide to receive you when you arrive. After a spell, once I've gotten to know you, I'll be able to guide you on to your very own hill, made just for you.

You might visit me soon, or I might have to wait for many, many years. No matter. Whenever you come, I'll be here to welcome you home.

Forever.

XX.

If only these damn merchants had kept on crying instead of blabbing to my mother. But no, they had to socialize, and now Mama's in my face asking why I bought another waterblanket.

"You already wasted our money on two for your friends," she says. "What's this one for?"

Spent is the word I would have used. *Invested* even.

She eyes me. "Where were you planning to sneak off to?"

"It's *my* money. I earned it."

"Dolores, we talked about this."

I cross my arms. She wouldn't be fussing at me if she knew what I could have used the money for instead. But then, if she knew I was thinking of buying a gun, she'd just squawk about that.

She sighs. "Honey, it's not just about the money—though these things are outrageously expensive…"

I hold my tongue because sassing her will only draw this out and delay me.

"Please," she says simply. "Tell me where you're going."

My mouth opens, but I've lost my words. She's asking me, not yelling, not ordering. Saying "please." Now I feel the truth tugging itself out of me, moving toward her like metal to a magnet. "It's E, Mama. I think they're in trouble."

I tell her about the email from Meena, strange rumors about an encampment of gargoyles dancing on a marble platform, turning everything to stone in the middle of the Nevada Desert.

"Weren't E and M already made of stone?" she asks.

"Yes."

"And they've found their other gargoyle friends."

"Yes."

"And the problem is…?"

"The problem is, other things—animals and things—are turning to stone as well. And… it looks like their encampment is growing."

"At the moment I'm more worried about the Gun Club." That's what we've been calling the table of armed men at the café. They've been coming in more frequently of late, murmuring lower. Angrier.

"Is this what they're riled up about?"

"I don't know, Dolores. But does it really matter?" Mama stares at me for a moment, then rubs her eyes. "I've spent so much of my life just trying to keep you safe, and now you want to go off and chase these gargoyles, running off by yourself with no protection—"

"I was going to get Ben to come with me."

Mama doesn't say a word, but she doesn't have to. She noticed when he stopped coming around, and has commented on how shady it was that he didn't say where he went. I told her he's probably undercover, but she didn't buy it. "I wanted to get the waterblankets now—"

"Blankets, plural?"

"—so we could head out as soon as he got back."

Her lips twist. "And if—whenever—he comes back, what if he doesn't want to go with you?"

Of course I've thought about that. I could just sit here and ignore whatever E's mixed up in, forget about all the living things turning to stone, that radius getting wider every day. Wait until it comes right up to our door.

But no, I can't.

"Then I'll find another way," I say.

She shakes her head, and I fold her into my arms and hug her tight. "I know you're worried about me. But this is too important not to do anything. People could get hurt."

Mama tsks, but doesn't pull away.

"I'll just go talk to them," I say. "I'm the closest thing they have to a friend. Maybe they'll listen."

She leans back to look me in the eye. "You think they will?"

"Maybe E will."

Actually, I'm not sure why they would, given the choice to be safe with their own kind. But I can't not try.

Mama wraps her arms around me and squeezes, tight. "I love you, is all."

"I love you too, Mama."

We hug each other full of strength for a bit, then she steps back and puts her hands on her hips. "All right, I think I could borrow Sarah's dune buggy."

"Who's Sarah?"

"She's a—regular. You've seen her, about my age, long salt-and-pepper hair, always gets breakfast for dinner."

"Oh, her."

Mama stares at the ground to concentrate. "When we get there, you'll need to talk to them without getting too close. So we'll need to be loud—we could borrow a—but that'll be trickier to—and we need to figure out—but I'll bet we could—"

I blink at the frequent use of "we" in Mama's rapid-fire, fragmentary planning.

"What?" she says. "We don't have to wait for *him*."

"Mama—"

She tips her head in that way that tells me her mind is made up.

"My sweet baby girl," she says, cradling my cheek in her palm. "You didn't think I'd let you do this alone, did you?"

I hug her again, partly to steady myself. Now that it seems more real, I'm more nervous than ever. "I guess we've got some planning to do."

"Well, we can't head out right away. I'm expecting a package, a laser attachment for my spear." She pats my cheek. "You didn't think you were the only one with her own private piggy bank, did you?"

FROM: Meena Gupta
TO: Manfred Himmelblau

Subject: Search Update/Report: In the City of Scheming Stones

Manfred, I think I know where Joseph is going, and I'm driving as fast as I can to get there. Take a look at the entry for Crater Lake. After his last report, it would make sense, but I hope I'm wrong.

Stopped for coffee so I wouldn't drive off the road. Here's a quick report, a bit sloppy, but you understand why.

Dictated from a Douglas fir (DF – yes, a tree) in Mt. Shasta, California via an ingenious electronic interface invented centuries ago in Grenoble, France (this is what the trees report, at least)

Location Notes: Mt. Shasta has changed quite a bit since we last came through. It's completely empty. Deserted. No one is left. The trees remain, but the few buildings that haven't been burned to the ground are abandoned, and the ground is littered with groupings of rocks spelling messages like "get out" and "stay away"

DF: They aren't necessarily evil, or even ill-mannered, these stones, though we understand how their actions might make that impression. But they didn't do what they did for power—at least not for power over anyone or anything else, just the power to determine their own fates. Call that power if you must; we call it freedom.

Yes, we're the trees everyone called "gun-toting" (though we would say "liberation-minded"), but that's not what this story is about. It's about the so-called "scheming" stones, whom we would prefer to call "organizing" or "self-actualizing," but that doesn't comport with human conceptions of the situation, and we all know how conceptually fragile you are, so we'll go ahead and keep telling the story under your title. But just know this: deep down, we don't consent to the intellectually impoverished boundaries of your worldview.

Back to our stones, then. We know humans find them "difficult," but we appreciate them. Admire them. We're grateful to them. After we were disarmed in that disastrous [redacted] raid (which, you may recall, raged way out of control, resulting in the fiery deaths of many of the citizens it was meant to have saved) we were left defenseless. Our trunks had barely stopped smoking when people in hardhats began poking around, so-called "officials" and "developers" talking about the best way to rebuild, debating whether any of us who had survived the fire should be spared.

As though that were up to *them*.

While they poked and prodded, we trees were holding our own discussions, planning how to re-arm ourselves in time to avoid whatever further destruction the humans had in mind. The stones, however, didn't simply plan; they leapt into action, flinging themselves at the human interlopers from all directions, pelting their helmets and jackets, rolling over their toes, knocking clipboards from hands, denting trucks, and generally throwing themselves into harm's way. In one instance of selfless heroism, a stone slammed itself through a windshield, shattering it, but landing inside the cab to be taken God knows where when the driver made his escape.

Yes, we believe in God. But They don't want the things you think They want. You'll see. Eventually.

After the initial attack, more people came to investigate, of course, which resulted in an even more gruesome rout. The stones don't seem to suffer fools lightly, and if people didn't learn that the first time, that's on them. They didn't tell us to tell you that, per se, we just saw what happened; and as little as we care about your welfare, we still find wholesale violence distasteful. We don't care to see yet another motley, bedraggled group of humans moaning and limping to their battered vehicles, or trying like last time to lift off in stone-punctured helicopters (seriously, what were they thinking?), so we're just passing along some friendly advice. No one needs your brand of chaos. Really. It's embarrassing.

In fact, we still get a little upset at what they said when they came to rebuild—they actually asked us to believe that we'd need *humans* to reestablish *ourselves*. Can you believe that? No, no, no, we'll be just fine, thank you. The stones will be too—they'd already anticipated the plan to use them to rebuild, since the townsfolk had stopped trusting "lumber." Faced with the task of building a city not even their own stupidity could burn down, humans wound up getting chased out by the very stones they thought they'd use as materials.

We love thinking back on that day the townsfolk came to us, after the second rout, wanting us to talk sense into the stones.

Really? we said. *You just assume that we all know each other because we all live outside? Like we all speak the same fanciful nature language or something? Wow. No, we don't automatically know them or their language. Do the labor, humans. Google something sometimes.*

LOL, of course we can speak to the stones. It was just fun to watch all those untethered humans stamping their feet when we refused to.

Look, all they can do now is accept it: this city no longer belongs to them, or any other human. You should all just save yourselves the heartbreak and move on. That silly name you gave this place, City of Gun-Toting Trees, is meaningless: you're now standing in the City of Scheming Stones.

And if we were you, we wouldn't linger.

XXI.

Day and night we dance in the City of Dancing Gargoyles. There is no music but that of our bodies, the clink of stone fur, the clack of jade scales, the thumping of feet and tails against the marble floor our movement has conjured from the sand.

M and I dance surrounded by our kind: an elephant lifts its carnelian trunk and flaps its wings, a tourmaline monkey beats the floor with bear-like claws, a moth made of agate flutters and flops to our tempo. We move among malachite bird-men, amethyst angels, all possible combinations of peacocks and lizards and lions and humans, dazzling in jasper and jade, ruby and turquoise, rose quartz and lapis lazuli.

We dance in unison. We don't even need to speak. We dance and we change things. When birds flutter too close, they harden and morph, clunking to the ground. A few moments later they rise, shining and new, to jolt and jitter along in our rhythm. Butterflies swoop low and crystallize, grow stone horns or human faces, then hop on new claws to our beat.

We are safe. We are together. We are dancing.

Our marble floor widens—slowly, but daily—and we turn more and more creatures into stone. M says we're freeing them. And I can't deny, I do feel free. For the first time since I've been alive, I don't feel thirst. I can bask in the warmth of the sun without worrying when the next rain will come. I no longer live in fear of drying up and crumbling into pieccs.

From time to time, I see a figure off in the distance, sometimes several. Men watching, well away from our perimeter. Even from a distance, I recognize the outlines of rifles strapped against their backs.

We're saving lives here, M says, and with patience, we can save even more.

Surely everyone wants to live free of worry, smooth and gleaming under the sun.

We are safe. We are together. We are dancing. Everyone deserves to be free from want.

And if we keep working together, he says, everyone will.

FROM: Manfred Himmelblau
TO: Meena Gupta

FWD: In the City of Sinking Ghosts

By god, Meena, you were right. Please hurry.

------------Forwarded Message-------------

FROM: Joseph Evans
TO: Manfred Himmelblau

Subject: In the City of Sinking Ghosts

Location: Crater Lake, Oregon

What do ghosts drown in?

Grief?

Vengeance?

Regret?

Those seem obvious answers, but none of them are true.

How do I know?

Because I have spent much time in the City of Sinking Ghosts. There is an ocean between here and there. And there are ferrymen—many, more than all the gondoliers in Venice. But it costs more than a coin from your mouth or two from your eyes to get across. And it's not as regulated as one would like to think. There are no posted rates, so the ferrymen charge whatever they want to.

Ghosts come from all directions, some in their finest suits and dresses, some in a puff of ashes, some clutching teddy bears or dolls, some with only their thumbs to suck on. None of them speak, but they all seem to know they have to cross the ocean. They line up on the shore, holding out their jewels, their gold, their moldering roses, offering whatever they have for however far it will get them.

The boats appear empty because the ferrymen are invisible until they extend a limb to accept a payment that appeals to them. An empty vessel will slip up to the bank and a palm will appear, or a paw will uncurl, or a talon will hover, ready to snatch a trinket out of a ghost's trembling hand. This is the only part of the ferryman a ghost will ever see, and they must decide whether to trust this unseen guide or risk another.

To signal assent, to transform from supplicant to passenger, all the ghost needs to do is drop their watch into the outstretched palm, or allow the paw to swipe their jewels, or hold their coins out for the talon to take.

But some ghosts are paralyzed by choice. Others don't have the proper currency to attract a ride. For whatever reasons, many ghosts simply wade down the slope and disappear into the inky water. They don't drown in the usual way. They can walk along the bottom of the ocean, completely submerged in the oily black currents, but for only so long. They must be quick.

When I see especially small ones begin that waterlogged journey, I follow them and push them along the ocean floor. Most of them don't make it, diffusing instead into ripples, becoming part of the threshold they attempted to cross. If they're light enough, I might be able to carry them, but all too often I step out onto the other shore with only the remnants of a ghost dripping down my arms.

Why do I do this? Why do I alone haunt the shores of here and thereafter waiting for the most despairing souls? Is it because I was one of the few to make it safely across? Because of the ease with which I traveled? Was I punished by an ancient god, cursed to perform this task for a thousand years? Was I delivered to this shore before I was destined to be here, perhaps before I was even born?

There is so much I do not know. But what I do know is this:

Ferries cross without ceasing.

And ghosts stream daily to the shore, many of them holding up all manner of riches, even more of them wading into the muck with scraps.

And with every ghost that drowns, the ocean inches higher.

And when it breaches the banks, there will be no salvation on either side.

XXII.

Mama stands atop Sarah's dune buggy, watching the skies through binoculars. I'm standing next to the vehicle on the crest of a sand dune, looking through binoculars at a bunch of shiny, multicolored gargoyles hopping on a huge marble disc. There are dozens and dozens of them. A hundred? Maybe more? There's a delay between their hopping and the *thunk* of stone on stone echoing across the desert.

While Mama searches the sky, I scan the sands—we can't assume the marble floor marks the border of transformation from flesh to stone.

"There," says Mama. I look up at another bird, frozen and plummeting. "About fifty yards out, like the lizards. That's our boundary."

She climbs down and slides into the passenger seat. I take my place in the driver's seat and clutch the wheel tight. Despite all my talk, I'm glad she's here with me.

I drive down the crest of the dune, closing the distance between us and the City of Dancing Gargoyles. About sixty yards out, I stop. Mama opens the bag of worms we gathered and chucks one ahead of us. Still a worm. I move us forward at a crawl, Mama throwing worms, until one of them falls with a thunk on the sand. It turns a pretty shade of purple, then after a few seconds, begins heading toward the gargoyles in a curious hopping dance.

I turn off the engine, and the *thunk* of their feet on marble fills the silence. I keep my eyes on the worm as it hops in time, because I can't bear the thought of looking up and seeing E, finding them changed.

Mama's voice snaps me back: "Ready?"

I bite my lip and nod.

We get out and lift a solar-powered speaker from the back seat of the dune buggy onto the bars of the roof. She flips a switch and it buzzes to life. I take a deep breath and turn the microphone on.

"E and M?"

The speaker squeals and I take a step to the side—not forward.

"Guess a bullhorn would have sufficed," says Mama.

I try again: "We're looking for the gargoyles E and M."

My heart hammers. A few missteps muddy the rhythm of gargoyle feet, but they don't stop dancing. It only takes a couple of beats for the pattern to resume as though nothing had happened.

"E and M, are you there?" I call out. "It's me, Dolores."

Mama tosses some worms out to test the border. We're still good.

"E, please, can I talk to you?"

I raise the binoculars and watch the jumping gargoyles for any sign of E in the mass of wings and horns and paws and scales and tails. I shudder at a glimpse of a human face chiseled from rose-colored stone set atop an owl's body.

Then I see who I'm looking for pressing through the scrum of gargoyles. E steps out of the crowd and hovers at the edge of it.

I step forward, but Mama stops me with a hand on my arm.

Right.

E's beautiful in the sunlight, a rich shade of green, glittery, polished, shining. But are they still *E*?

I let the binoculars dangle on the strap around my neck, clear my throat, and speak into the microphone. "E, are you okay? Can I talk to you?"

They look back into the crowd, then to me, but don't move.

"E, I…"

Where do I even start? How do I tell someone they might be in a cult that's about to destroy the world—over a portable speaker on a dune buggy?

"Try the story, honey," says Mama.

It was my idea, because E likes stories, but now it seems dumb. Still…

"E, can I tell you a story?" They don't come closer, but they don't leave either, so I pull out my sheets of paper and begin: "Remember my friend Meena? The one who visits all those places? This is something she shared with me, one of her interviews. She thought I might like it, and I thought you might like it, so… This is called 'In the Garden of Rings': *Mama's always told me—*

"This isn't me and *my* Mama, by the way," I clarify. "It's just a story.

"*Mama's always told me not to try planting a ring on my own. I've watched her thrust her hands into the dirt for years now, loosening the soil, shaping a hole, then rummaging through her little box of rings for one to bury. Even now, she only lets me watch, never telling me exactly what she's wishing for with each ring. Even though I'm grown enough to help with all the other chores around the house. Even after I became a woman myself in that messy, red way about which she simply said, 'Well, here we go,' before handing me a pad.*

"*Mama's tight-lipped about most things, but especially the rings. It's like she's jealous of anyone else having her power; and I suppose she is, since she went to the trouble to grow a dragon to watch over our farm.*

"See, you can tell that's not *my* Mama," I say. "There's no way she'd want a dragon that close.

"*All Mama's ever shared is that she can only have three ring-wishes at a time, and she's not trading in the house or the dragon, so she only has the one crop a year to play with. One free wish at a time, that's why I'm not to touch her box of rings.*

"*Each spring she plants a ring and we watch it grow—me, eager to find out what her wish is, and her, anxious to see what it will actually look like. One year a whole field of corn sprouted from a yellow solitaire diamond ring, each ear of corn studded with pearls instead of kernels, except for the one that held another ring. Mama put that ring in her box and sold most of the pearls. We made enough to feed ourselves and the dragon, and still add to our nest egg in the bank. Mama kept the ones she didn't sell in an inflatable pool in the basement for the dragon to watch over, and sometimes when she was in a good mood we'd step in and splash around in our own little sea of pearls.*

"Not anymore, though, now that I'm grown. She says she's keeping them for my future. Funny, though: when I tried to take one to give to my friend past the edge of the farm, the dragon didn't let me out of the house."

I look up from my papers. E has stepped a little closer, off the marble into the sand. Mama's keeping an eye on the worms. Still good.

"Another year, a ruby ring grew into a single pomegranate tree. Our dragon wrapped itself around that tree, and we spent the summer picking the plump red fruits, splitting their skins open and scooping dozens of diamonds out of sticky crimson pulp. Still, Mama didn't really relax until we opened the fruit that held another ring. No matter that the ring box was never empty; Mama couldn't truly enjoy the harvest until it produced one more seed for the future. She insisted on finding it, even the year she grew the dragon.

"I was still small that year, maybe ten, but I'll never forget watching her plant the emerald ring, then gawking in amazement week after week as the tips of the beast's horns sprouted. As it continued to grow, earth fell away from the scaly skin of its forehead, until one day it finally opened its eyes and trained those glistening red orbs on me. Mama'd rush out to the fields every time it breathed fire, searching the previous year's scorched stalks for a flash of metal or a glittering stone. Turns out we just had to be patient, then hold our noses and sift. I hate to think how many dungpiles we soiled ourselves with— me, at my age, barely taller than the piles—before the ring finally emerged."

When I look up this time, E's even closer. Mama squints at the worms on the sand. They're starting to shrivel. She throws a fresh one out to double-check. Still good.

"After that, I thought she'd finally be a little less tense, less guarded with a dragon to do the guarding for us. I couldn't have put it into words then, but I guess I hoped I'd finally get a mother who could focus on me for a change, rather than watching out for the neighbors or fingering through that ring box mulling over what to wish for next. I know she was just looking out for me, in her own way, but I always felt kind of like an afterthought. Even then I had the sense I wasn't something she'd specifically wished for. I was never one of her rings.

"But now I'm grown, in that red, messy way we never really discussed, and there's someone else out there, someone Mama doesn't know about, who makes me feel like I was wished right down from the stars. I've been going out to meet this someone past the edge of the farm, beyond anyplace our dragon even cares about, and I've been telling this girl every wish I have, about exploring the big wide world, and finding a home, a real home with love and hugs and kisses, arms around one another, eyes closed for a moment of peace and contentment."

This time when I look up, I note that a black marble lion with wings has emerged from the crowd and is now listening and watching from the edge of the marble disk. I gasp at M's transformation.

Mama's keeping an eye on both the gargoyles and the worms.

I swallow and continue: *"I asked Mama last night what she was going to plant this spring. She told me not to worry my little head about it, that she and the dragon would decide. Her eyes gleamed red in the hearth fire as she explained how I'd understand one day, when this farm was mine and I had a child of my own to protect. Her bony fingers gripped the ring box like claws."*

E's even closer now—but so is M.

"So now I'm off to plant my own ring. Not one from Mama's box—the dragon almost snapped off my hand when I tried to take one in the wee hours of the morning. Same for the pearls that were supposedly for my future. But the dragon didn't seem to care at all when I left with a bag slung over my shoulder holding my two favorite dresses, a change of shoes, and a bit of food to last until whatever happens next."

E's just a few steps away.

"*I won't forget Mama's advice: I won't plant a ring on my own. I will wear my love's ring, and she'll wear mine, and we'll find our own plot of land, dig our hands into the dirt, and grow our own future. Together.*"

That's it. The end. I turn off the mic and wait.

The stomping of gargoyles pulses behind E. All of them could turn on us at any moment, while I'm standing here waiting for—what?

E smiles, that familiar sight newly dazzling in green. "So, are you saying you're in love with me?"

I blink.

E bursts into laughter, and after a beat, so do I. I've missed that laugh, and I'm relieved that it hasn't changed. "How are you?" I ask. "Are you okay?"

"*We're* fine," says M, padding into place beside E. He sits and stares directly at me, flicking his tail. "We're better than fine, thank you. Yourselves?"

"Concerned," says Mama, now right beside me.

I clench my teeth; there goes our plan to start light. But with M sitting there smirking, nothing feels like the right thing to say. "More like 'curious.' Like, what's all this?" I ask, gesturing at the gargoyles behind them. "What are you guys up to?"

I'm looking at E, but M answers: "Dancing. Care to join?"

"Don't!" E yells, with an edge in their voice I've never heard before.

"It's true, then," I say. "You're doing this; transforming things." I glance at M before focusing back on E. "Expanding."

"We're making things better," E says. "Everyone will be free from hunger and thirst." But despite the change in E's tone, I can still read their face. I see the doubt there.

M stands up again and hovers next to E, reminding me of all the men I've seen loom over us, all the bosses who've tried to intimidate Mama and me into working for peanuts. All the assholes who want to control the world.

"Then maybe we *should* join you," I say, and take a step forward. Mama grabs my arm.

E rears up and holds their front legs out toward me. "Stop!"

"Why?" I ask.

They stare at me, frozen. I stare back, heart thundering in my chest in time with the thumping of a hundred gargoyles.

Finally, M nudges E, then turns and walks away. "Come on," he says over his shoulder. "We have work to do."

E blinks, then turns—but just to the side. They're wavering.

"I'll come back tomorrow," I say. "With another story."

They look down to check the length of their shadow. "This same time?"

"This same time."

E smiles.

FROM: Meena Gupta
TO: Manfred Himmelblau
CC: Joseph Evans

Subject: On the Island of Drowning Paintbrushes

Location: Wizard Island, Crater Lake, Oregon

Joseph, if you can read this, please say something. I'm here, but I can't see you, and it seems you can't hear me calling out for you.

You've got to be here somewhere.

Wizard Island is an island of failure. A place of muddied colors, of compositions that weren't quite right, an island of done-for-now-but-not-great. Land of *I'll come back later, I'll do better next time.*

This is also an island of cleansing, of satisfaction with a job well done, of moving ahead to a new phase. A place of *it's-all-complete, it's perfect.*

And this is an island of paintbrushes, brushes that have drowned, some slipping directly from a hand into the water, others sliding away unnoticed, never to be seen again. Many are grizzled and blown, with bent, shaggy bristles, broken and frayed. A few are still sleek and new, haunted by the voices of the people still looking for them on the other side of the water. So much they hadn't yet gotten to paint.

All manner of paintbrushes wash up on this island: thick ones, plumper than the fingers of the children who held them; elegant ones with sleek synthetic fibers; wide, battered commercial-use brushes, speckled with all the colors they've been plunged into to create murals or paint houses. These are the lucky ones, the ones that slip away while their painters still want them around. These brushes were still of use, lost during cleaning rather than thrown into the garbage or stuffed into a dusty old drawer.

There's no way to know who opens the portal, or when, or why. All that can be said for sure is that the brushes fall through a glass jar of turpentine or a bucket of water, slipping past some unknown membrane into a void before they wash up on this shore, saturated and carrying their own distinct odors, say, a whiff of natural horsehair or traces of solvent.

Many of these brushes arrive with a shimmy of relief, relating stories of increasing frustration with their own performance. They tell how their painters had shaken them dry with flicks of the wrist, agitated, smoothing their bristles with extra force, examining them with increasing skepticism. These brushes had a sense their days were numbered—is this perhaps how it happened? Was it premonition that prevented them from being planted handle-first into the coffee can paintbrush graveyard, to be forgotten forever? Did sheer will for a new life allow them to sink into the liquid abyss, deeper and deeper, down and away until they churned into the surf and sank into the soft sands of this shore—their new home?

In what world is wanting a change enough to make it? And what of all those who still had so much more to contribute back in their original worlds? People are still searching for answers, here on the Island of Drowning Paintbrushes. No one knows why the paintbrushes come, and no one has figured out how to predict which brushes will contribute themselves to the vocational school or the art league supply cabinet in their new home, eager to help paint fences or spruce up ceramics, versus those who will simply stand with their handles in the sand and watch the waves lap in and out, day after day.

No one seems to know how long the brushes will stay, only that at some point they will decide it's time to go. It could be while working on a landscape, dotting a fleck of sunlight on a leaf, or turning a window shutter teal, or watching the thousandth tide roll in. At some point each brush will decide it's needed elsewhere and hop out into the surf, never to be seen again.

Do the brushes go back to their original owners? Do they turn up on a new shore? Is there a heaven just for paintbrushes? I don't know. All I know is what comes from the waves must return there.

As one resident told me, "Our drowning paintbrushes aren't ours to keep. We must simply be glad they helped us for a while."

Do you see? They go where helpers go. That's where I'm going too.

So Joseph, when I come, help me find you.

I'm almost there.

XXIII.

First we dug. Now we dance. We don't suffer from heat or thirst. We never tire. We send our drumbeat of stone against stone out into the world, waiting for more gargoyles to find us. With every lizard that freezes, every bird that drops from the sky, our numbers grow, our radius expands.

Dolores and her mother came twice more before they had to go back home. Before she left, she told me the story of a gargoyle on a journey from the middle of a thumping desert to a city with an echoing church. A sweet story, but that church will remain empty—they have their own lives, among their own people. We have our own lives among ours.

Still, sometimes when I notice a certain slant of the shadows, I wonder if Dolores will come with another story. I squeeze through the crowd to the edge of our expanding disc and wait. She never comes.

It's one of those afternoons, and I'm waiting for the usual nothing when I see—something. My heart beats faster as two forms approach, rippling in the heat on the horizon. My smile falters when I realize it's not Dolores and Rose, but then a new slightly anxious excitement hits me when I realize what they are.

"Gargoyles!" I yell, turning back to the dancing. "More gargoyles!"

A few gargoyles near the edge of our enclave turn toward the new arrivals, and we walk out to greet them. The rest keep on dancing. There is still work to do, after all.

As we get closer, I note that the new ones are both carved like serpents. I wonder if they could have been created by the same human as I was.

A winged, blue-star-sapphire minotaur strides past me to reach them first. "Welcome! We're so pleased you found us. Where are you coming from?"

"We just arrived from Middlegate," says the one on the left. "Strange things going on there."

"Like what?" I ask, eager for a new story.

They smile and look at one another, eyes full of mischief. But before they can respond, they cross our threshold, and their scales go iridescent, turning from rough alabaster to sparkling opal.

Their gazes shift, their attention now fixed on the dancing behind us. The minotaur sweeps a beckoning hand toward our enclave, and the impromptu welcoming party escorts them to our growing disc. I see M at the edge, nodding his welcome to the new gargoyles. Even after they pass, he remains there. He's watching me, waiting for me to return.

We stare at each other. He finally steps off the disc and saunters toward me, his obsidian form moving smoothly over the sand. With each step, sunlight glints off the white seams running through his black marble. When he reaches me, he sits.

"What troubles you?" he asks.

I can only shake my head and look past him toward our enclave, where the new gargoyles have already been absorbed. Subsumed.

M sighs. "You can't stop it, you know. It's for the best anyway."

"Is it?" I focus on him once more, dismayed by his placid expression. "Are they—are we—really even gargoyles anymore?"

"Are any of those broken piles of rubble we left behind gargoyles anymore?"

As callous as his words are, his tone isn't cruel. For him, it's merely fact. They are dead, we are—technically—not.

"We've adapted, E. Something your human friends need to learn. Regardless, it's going on all around them, and will continue to do so whether they choose to join it or not."

I shake my head. "We can't—"

"We can and we are. Haven't you been paying attention? Isn't it as I've said? We're dancing, the dinosaurs are dancing, the bonfires are dancing, the wolves and the trees and the devils are dancing. Butterflies and statues and bats are dancing. The very stones of the earth have begun dancing—all of them in their own way."

"But how do you know? They can't all be like us, can they?" I struggle against a dark vision forming inside me. "They can't all want to destroy everything that isn't them."

M reaches out and puts a paw on my foot. "It's not about destruction, dear friend. It's about survival. And evolution." He pats my foot reassuringly, his marble clicking against my malachite, then saunters toward the other gargoyles. A few steps in, he turns and looks back at me over his shoulder. "She's human, E. And because she's human, she's vulnerable. It would have been so easy for that young man to hurt her."

"Did you kill him?" I shoot back.

He turns fully to face me. He doesn't have to say anything. I feel like I'm sinking.

"That's why they think we're monsters," I tell him.

"Didn't you want her to be safe? Perhaps what we're doing here will let her become something more resilient. Something you'll never have to worry about again."

The shush of M's footsteps fades as he walks away, and I think about all the changes we've seen, and what more could be out there, all the things that could be dancing their own brands of chaos into the world. What if M's right? What if it's not merely destruction? What if we're just part of some larger wave of evolution, alterations that are in turn altering the world?

But what about Dolores and her mother, and the pastor who was kind enough to let us stay in his church, and all the people who offered to help us find the City of Dancing Gargoyles. Can they adapt? Where would they fit into this new world?

I'm about to turn back toward my enclave when I glimpse something else on the horizon. I squint against the sun. Something is flapping in the breeze—like human clothing. I start out toward it, feeling hopeful but also stupid for hoping it's her. Whoever it is, better to catch them before they cross over into stone.

The fabric is flapping, but the figure doesn't seem to be moving. Odd. I keep walking toward it.

Then I recognize the glint: a waterblanket, hanging on a creosote bush. Also stuck to the bush is a map, no words, just a series of arrows pointing from a big disc in the desert, around a scrubland, to a town with a church. Inside the church is a bowl of water with a cinnamon stick and a smiley face. And a heart.

I look back at M and all the other gargoyles dancing in the distance, and ask myself: What is the point of a dance when there is no joy? What is the point of a story when there's no one to share it with?

I pluck the waterblanket off the bush, and wrap it around myself and wonder:

What is the purpose of a creature created for rain when there is no more rain?

Crater Lake

Joseph?
Joseph, I'm here. Where are you?
I can't believe the water is so clear. It's beautiful. But it's cold.
I'm so cold.

Meena.

Joseph? Is that you? I can't see you.

Not Joseph.

Who is this?

Keep going, you'll find him.

Who are you?
Are you one of the ghosts?
Hello?

Not a ghost. Keep going.

I'm so cold. Is this a dream?
This has to be a dream.

What did you think would happen when you walked into the lake?

I—I don't know. I just thought…
I just thought I'd find him.

You trusted.

Yes.

In what exactly?
In the lake?

I don't know.
Who is this?

Keep going. Don't you see him now?

Yes. Joseph! Joseph!
Why can't he hear me?

He's still too far away.

Is that—a ghost in his arms?

What's left of one. Another one that won't make it.

Joseph!
I'm so cold…

Keep going, he can't hear you yet.

Who are you?

Look down.

I don't see anything.

Look.

Just—what is this I'm walking through? It's spongy.

Peat moss.

Okay… Is that…?

Yes, that's us.

What's going on?

It's part of your training.

Did Manfr—

Not Manfred.

Then who?

Do you still trust?

Well, I'm still breathing.
Joseph!

He's all right. He's just crying. He lost another one.

Joseph! Wait, why can't I move? Let me go.

In a moment.

Let go of my feet!

In a moment. You'll be fine as long as you continue to trust.

Good.

You and Joseph will be all right.

You'll wake, and you'll remember this as a dream,

but you'll know it's the truth.

What are you talk—

Keep researching, Meena. This is all part of your preparation.

For what? Who's doing this?

You'll find out if you keep seeking, we promise.

We're sorry our introduction has to be so—opaque. But it's for the best.

Now, go to Joseph. When you wake up, remember what we said.

Because we trust you too, Meena Gupta.

XXIV.

I watch Mama out of the corner of my eye, trying not to be too obvious. She's behind the counter, leaning on her palms and talking to Sarah. It's not unusual to see her talking to Sarah, but what's caught me by surprise is that they're *flirting*, and with a level of familiarity that tells me this isn't exactly a new development.

How could I not have noticed what was brewing between them? This is how oblivious I've been, wrapped up in my own drama.

Mama looks over at me, and I quickly switch my focus to the table I'm wiping.

A minute later, she's at my side, and we both watch Sarah head out the door. "You realize you've been wiping the same table for the past five minutes?" Mama says.

I offer a small, sheepish smile. "So... Sarah."

"Yeah, Sarah," says Mama. "We were thinking we could all grab dinner tonight, somewhere other than here. You in?"

It seems sudden, but I remind myself that's just because I haven't been paying attention. "Sure."

"Great. I think you'll like each other."

Mama looks so content, I get over my awkwardness and raise my chin. "I'm sure I'll approve of her."

"Smartass. Get back to work." Her step is light as she heads back into the kitchen.

It's weird to think about Mama dating, but she deserves some happiness. I can't keep dumping all my problems on her. But who else can I talk to? E's gone—we failed with them. And Ben…

Ben's the problem I would talk to E about, if they were here. Ben's still not back, and I keep hearing rumors about his side hustle, the things he was supposedly selling: weapons, drugs, worse—women. I feel sick when I think about all the signs I ignored. I mean, he offered to sell me a gun for god's sake.

I cringe every time I think about how dumb I was. How dumb I still am, because part of me wants him to come back and explain, tell me the rumors aren't true, that it's not him, that it's just his cover.

Another part of me is afraid he'll come back and admit it's all true. Even what they say about the women—some of them my age. Some younger.

I try to push it all out of my mind to go wait on a table. But I can't concentrate, and I wind up having to ask them to repeat their orders. It's a good thing it's not busy right now.

I stick the order in the wheel and am about to go refill waters when Mama calls my name. She's holding up another ticket I wrote, barely legible with scratched out lines and scribbled corrections. "You okay?"

"Yeah, just a little distracted."

As far as Mama's concerned, it's goodbye and good riddance with Ben, over and finished. But I can't let go of it.

Part of me refuses to believe what they say he's done. And then I feel angry that he's ignoring me, and then I feel stupid for being angry because I should be glad to be out of his orbit.

Another part of me wants him dead.

Mama tells me to knock off early, she'll handle it. But I don't, because the last thing I want is to be alone with this hamster wheel in my head.

I'm walking by the "Gun Club" table when I hear some disturbing talk about "surveilling the gargoyles." They don't seem to care who hears now—I suppose they think they're being heroic, and why hide that, right? I linger for a moment, eavesdropping while pretending to clean another table. But the talk isn't specific. No concrete plans—not yet. Just a roiling mess of insults and griping, peppered with "we should" and other vague threats. It doesn't take long for me to reach my limit. I toss my rag behind the counter and step outside to get away from their noise.

Outside, I lean against the wall in the slanted shade of late afternoon. I tilt my head back and close my eyes. Maybe if I could focus on a problem I might actually be able to solve, I'd feel less scattered. I can't solve Ben, but maybe I could take another crack at E before anyone decides to start a war.

Even on foot, E should have been able to find their way back by now. Either they're ignoring the waterblanket and map I left behind, or they haven't found them yet. Or M found the things and destroyed them. So how do I get to E without M interfering?

And how do I do it without asking Mama to put her life on hold again?

My eyes pop open: I'll write to Meena. She could help.

"Dolores?"

I turn my head in the direction of a familiar voice. The sun glints off a waterblanket, and I squint. I must be hallucinating.

Joy wells up inside me as the figure comes into view.

"I was hoping I'd find you here," says E.

I run toward them, but then stop cold. They're still that glittery green color underneath the waterblanket, which means—

"It's okay," they say. "I won't turn you to stone; I tested it on the way here. It's only the area around the enclave that's dangerous."

I sigh with relief and hug them so tight, water squeezes from the blanket onto my shirt. "Oh my god E, it's so good to see you. Are you okay? Do you need to rest? Come inside out of the heat—no, actually, it's probably best you don't. Sit down, I have so much to tell you." I know I'm babbling, but I'm so excited to see them I can't stop.

I lead E toward shade around the corner, where they shrug off the blanket. "It's good to be back, but…" They sit down, part sprawled on the sidewalk, part leaning against the wall. "Dolores, I'm worried. It's all moving so quickly."

I swallow and sit next to them. "The enclave."

"Yes. It's growing so fast. I don't know what to do." Their tail twitches nervously. "I'm sorry, I haven't even asked how you're doing."

"I'm fine; don't worry about it." Not strictly true, but my problems are hardly the biggest at the moment.

"How's Rose?" they ask.

"In love. Which reminds me." I check my watch and stand up. "We've got to hurry."

"Where are we going?" E asks, also standing.

"To figure out what to do next." I fold the waterblanket and drape it over my arm. "I'll drop this inside real quick. We've got to get to the library and email Meena before dinner with Mom and Sarah—you'll like her, though I don't really know her that well yet, but if Mama likes her, I'm sure both of us will."

I pull at my damp shirt, fanning it ineffectually. "Do I have time to change? I'll probably dry off by dinner. I wonder if Sarah will let us use her dune buggy again. I mean, to get out to the enclave. Although I didn't want to keep bothering Mama with all this. No, better to start with Meena."

E just stands there looking stunned. I hug them again and run inside with the waterblanket. I've got things to do, no time to explain.

Just how I like it.

XXV.

The City of Dancing Gargoyles has grown. I can't believe how many of us live there now.

Sarah stops her dune buggy at the top of the crest, and I lean my head out the side to get a better look. Rose sits in the passenger seat, and Dolores is in the back next to me, holding a bucket of fresh worms.

I watch my enclave dance down below, glittering and beautiful in the sunlight. Their thumping reverberates through clear, dry air like a stone heartbeat. It's only been a couple of weeks since I left, I think, but the numbers have swelled. There could be two hundred of us dancing below. The disc is certainly bigger, so I'm guessing the transformation radius has grown as well. How far away do living things have to stay now to avoid being turned to stone?

Dolores taps me to get my attention. She points out a cluster of tents on another crest to our left, well away from the disc. About a dozen men in tactical gear are milling around or sitting in camp chairs under portable shades—and most of them are looking our way.

This is why we're here. Rumors about gargoyles have been rampant back in Carson City. Some say they've been attacking the militia camped out here, flying overhead, snatching them up and into the enclave. People call their dancing satanic, or say they were sent over here from another country to wreak havoc. Of course, nobody's been officially declared missing, injured, or dead, but that doesn't stop people from stoking fears.

Between that, and the whispers going around the café about procuring additional ammo and "other supplies," we couldn't afford to wait for Meena.

"Okay, you ready?" asks Sarah.

I ask her to wait.

Rose turns to face me. "It's okay, E. I recognize some of those men from the café. You'll be all right with us."

"No, it's just that—I don't want them to know how close they can get to the enclave." I hop down from the dune buggy. "Maybe they've already figured it out, but if not..."

"No, I get it," says Dolores. Then, to her mother and Sarah: "The farther we keep E from those guys, the better. E can go on ahead to find M while we talk to the militia."

"Militia," scoffs Sarah. "Just a bunch of frightened men."

"Well, I can't say I entirely blame them." Rose is looking down at the enclave through binoculars. "If I didn't know E, I wouldn't know what to think about all that down there either."

If gargoyles could blush, I would. I never thought I'd hear something that sounded like trust from Rose. Dolores gives me a thumbs up, grinning. A comforting warmth blooms inside me as I turn and head down toward the enclave. I scurry close to the ground so as not to be noticeable—or as threatening to the armed men Sarah begins driving toward.

The closer I get to my City, the more confused I feel. These are my kind—so why am I so nervous?

I move closer still, and the vibration of our dancing settles in my body. We have a right to exist. And yet, I have to tell the enclave to exist differently, just because humans are afraid of us. Because they don't understand.

But then I remind myself that I'm here to talk M out of his ambitions of expansion. Humans aren't scared of us because they don't understand us. It's because they understand us all too well.

I look up at the militia tents just as Sarah's dune buggy reaches them. No one's pointing guns at anyone.

Yet.

I turn back to the gargoyles—my gargoyles—and notice curious glances from dancers at the edge of the disc. Now I'm the new arrival, which makes me feel awkward all over again, until I see some familiar gargoyles: the star-sapphire minotaur, the opal serpents, the man-faced owl.

And M.

He's trying to hide his surprise, then his pleasure, as he saunters toward me. When I tilt my head as though to say *Really?* he abandons all pretense and trots to close the distance between us.

"E, it's good to see you!"

When he sniffs me to make sure I'm all right, I want to cry. I stand on my rear legs and drape myself around him in a hug. I hear other gargoyles gathering around us, some of them asking who I am, others patting my back, welcoming me home.

Home.

Is it possible for a gargoyle to have more than one of those?

M pulls back and beams at me proudly. "I see you changed your mind. You came back."

I open my mouth for a moment, not wanting to say it. But I have to. "Not exactly."

M's expression stiffens. He tells the others they can get back to dancing, that we'll catch up with them. Then we walk to the edge of the disc and look up at the humans on the crest. He sits on his haunches, and I settle in next to him.

"We can't ignore that," I say, nodding up to the people.

"Oh, we're not."

I shake my head, exasperated. "That's the problem. They can see you're expanding. And the bigger you get, the more men they'll send out here. Then they'll start shooting."

"They already have," he snarls. "Come with me."

He rises, and I follow him into the hopping crowd, weaving through winged, hooved, and horned creatures glistening in more colors than I could ever imagine. We thread through our dancing compatriots until we reach a less densely-populated area toward the center. Dancers have made room for three gargoyles lying on the marble: a ruby gryphon, a jade bear, and a wolf with a serpent's head.

M's growling now, and when I get close to them, I see why. Their bodies are peppered with chips and holes.

"Bullet holes," he mutters.

My head feels light. "What happened?"

"One of the men came too close and got frightened by something— who knows, maybe he saw a lizard turn to stone in front of him. Whatever it was, he just started shooting into the crowd. Azar, Burdick, and Fen were able to run him off, but this was the price."

I flop down wearily next to M. "Are they going to be okay?"

"We don't know. This is all new. For everyone."

For just one moment I allow myself to imagine M flying me over the men's encampment, then letting me drop down amongst their tents to squeeze the life out of every last one of them.

But no, that kind of thinking is exactly the problem. I have to be calm.

"M." I hesitate. "We have to talk to them."

"They've already spoken," he says, nodding at the injured gargoyles. "Violence is the only language they know."

"No, that's not true. Think about Dolores. And remember the pastor who let us stay in his church? And..." My list of humans who have treated us decently is pitifully short, but I scrounge up a new one. "And guess what: Rose actually trusts me now."

M huffs skeptically.

"Really," I press. "How do you think I got here? She and Dolores and Sarah—"

"Who's Sarah?"

"I'll explain later. But they want to help. They're up there talking to the militia right now."

I get back on my feet and stand next to M, side by side, looking down at our pock-marked friends. "You know Dolores would be as angry as we are about this."

He huffs again, but less sharply.

"And you remember how tenacious she is, right? If anyone could wear down those men, it would be her."

M shakes his head, but a low chuckle escapes him.

"But first, we'd have to pause. As the humans say, take a breath, deescalate."

"As the humans say," he growls. "Why should we do anything as the humans say?"

"Because as bad as this is, they can do worse. And they will." I turn to him, try to read his reaction. "They're preparing to right now. And we could stop it all by just—taking a breath."

M stares straight ahead, frowning. Finally he asks, "And this 'taking a breath,' what would this entail?"

I sigh and lean against him. "Stopping the dancing."

He grunts, and I can feel the vibration.

"Just temporarily," I say. "Just long enough to calm everyone down."

"And what happens after this 'calming down'?"

I pause. "Honestly, I don't know."

M continues staring forward, a low rumble in his throat.

EPILOGUE

FROM: Manfred Himmelblau
TO: Dolores Baker
CC: Meena Gupta

Subject: Welcome!

Dear Dolores and E,

Thank you for your time on the phone yesterday. As I mentioned, I was impressed with your background, and your ongoing negotiations with the City of Dancing Gargoyles. I would be delighted to offer both of you positions as Envoys and Traveling Researchers for *The Annals of Alchemical Changes* (previously *The Annals of Alchemical Testing*).

While we have secured additional funding for your services as Envoys, appropriations take time, so you will serve under the Traveling Researcher classification in the meantime. Please refer to the attached report for reference to previous work in this area. As we discussed, you do not need to replicate this level of detail, as your work as Traveling Researchers will be secondary to your assignments as Envoys. We appreciate your ongoing mediation efforts to maintain the security of the City of Dancing Gargoyles while negotiating its growth. With luck, this may become a model for many future Envoy-ships across the West.

Once you confirm acceptance—and I hope you will—Meena Gupta will meet you at our new field office in Carson City to requisition your supplies. Your sand-powered vehicle will be provided via a beta-testing partnership with HuskCorp (yes, some compromises must be made), so please don't forget to log your user experiences.

Meena will be available to train you while her previous traveling companion is convalescing. You will be in excellent hands: it was due to her incredibly brave and selfless actions that he survived, and I'm pleased to say he is well on the way to recovery.

I realize that this may sound daunting, but I do wish to be completely candid about the risks. This is the reason we forbid our researchers to travel alone. But with a friendship like yours, I doubt either of you will ever have to travel alone again.

With the Sincerest of Welcomes,

Manfred

Dr. Manfred Himmelblau
Director, Citizens' Alchemical Realities Exchange (CARE)

Attachments: Appointment Letter_Baker_E.PDF, In the City of Failing Knives.PDF

Acknowledgments

I'll start where the book started: with Michael Moorcock's "deliberate paradoxes" novel pre-writing exercise, and the Matt Bell newsletter that introduced me to it. Thank you both for sparking the journey!

So many people have helped me find my way through these fantastical cities, but I owe special thanks to my writing groups: Write Club (Myna Chang, Marcy Dilworth, Mary Sophie Filicetti, Raima Larter, Raegan O'Lone, Jessica Seigel, and Beth Wenger) and Em-Dash (Matthew Bukowski, Yohanca Delgado, Cristi Donoso, Derrick Jefferson, Karen Keating, Molly McGinnis, and Bron Treanor). Thank you as well to my superstar beta readers: Myna, Marcy, Mary Sophie, Raima and Kristina Saccone. It's been an honor to work with and learn from all of you.

The DC-area literary community has been an incredibly supportive place to live and create. Thank you to the DC Commission on the Arts and Humanities for its generous and long-standing support of artists of all genres. Much love to the Barrelhouse fam, The Writer's Center community, and the American University MFA community for cheering me on along the way.

Thank you to the following journals for previously publishing versions of some of the stories in this book: *34 Orchard, Alternating Current, AntipodeanSF, Archive of the Odd, The Daily Drunk, Daily Science Fiction, Flash Frog, Gargoyle, Gigantic Sequins, HAD, Harpy Hybrid, If There's Anyone Left, Janus Literary, The Jarnal (Mason Jar), Jellyfish Review, Longleaf Review, Middle House Review, Nightlight, Paranoid Tree, Star*Line, Simultaneous Times, Starward Shadows Quarterly, Wizards in Space,* and *Wyldblood Magazine.*

Robert Llewellyn's photographs in Darlene Trew Crist's book *American Gargoyles: Spirits in Stone* provided fantastic visual inspiration for E and M and their whole crew. And, of course, huge gratitude to

Andrew Gifford and Monica Prince at SFWP for believing in this book, and to my editor Adam al-Sirgany for posing just the right questions at just the right points in time to nudge it into its best possible form. I owe you the world's biggest cinnamon stick.

About the Author

Tara Campbell is a writer, teacher, Kimbilio Fellow, fiction co-editor at Barrelhouse, and graduate of American University's MFA in Creative Writing. Previous publication credits include *Masters Review*, *Wigleaf*, *Electric Literature*, *CRAFT Literary*, *Daily Science Fiction*, *Uncharted Magazine*, *Strange Horizons*, and *Escape Pod/Artemis Rising*. She's the author of a novel (*TreeVolution*), two hybrid collections of poetry and prose (*Circe's Bicycle* and *Political AF: A Rage Collection*), and two short story collections (*Midnight at the Organporium* and *Cabinet of Wrath: A Doll Collection*). *City of Dancing Gargoyles* is her sixth book. Find her online at www.taracampbell.com

Also from Santa Fe Writers Project

Strange Folk You'll Never Meet
by A.A. Balaskovits

From the author of the best-selling *Magic For Unlucky Girls* comes a new collection of magical short stories with a fabulist feminist edge...

> "Exquisite...This accomplished collection interlocks the horrific and the wondrous through deliciously dry humor, resulting in a unique must-read for fans of Angela Carter, Maria Dahvana Headley, and A.S. Byatt."
>
> — *Publishers Weekly*

Horse Show *by Jess Bowers*

Bowers' quirky and fascinating short story collection explores how humans have loved, abused, and spectacularized their equine companions through American history, photography, and film. These 13 slim stories take us from the shocking tale of P.T. Barnum's "mammoth" horse to the tragicomic fate of Wilbur's neglected wife in the TV show Mr. Ed.

> "Highly original...quirky, fascinating, easy to read and hard to forget."
>
> — Madison Smartt Bell, National Book Award and PEN/ Faulkner Finalist, author of the *All Souls Rising* trilogy

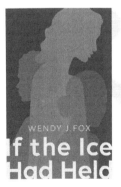

If the Ice Had Held *by Wendy J. Fox*

Melanie Henderson's life is a lie. The scandal of her birth and the identity of her true parents is kept from her family's small, conservative Colorado town. Not even she knows the truth: that her birth mother was just 14 and unmarried to her father, a local boy who drowned when he tried to take a shortcut across an icy river.

> "Razor-sharp...written with incredible grace and assurance."
>
> — Benjamin Percy, author of *The Dark Net*

About Santa Fe Writers Project

SFWP is an independent press founded in 1998 that embraces a mission of artistic preservation, recognizing exciting new authors, and bringing out of print work back to the shelves.

 @santafewritersproject | @SFWP | sfwp.com